MISTRESS OF DESIRE

An Awakening of Desire

RUBY SCOTT

Ruby Scott

www.rubyscott.com

Want a free book?

Get a free sapphic romance book when you sign up to my newsletter today!

Just click here to subscribe

A thought... or Two

"The most difficult thing is the decision to act, the rest is merely tenacity."

- Amelia Earhart

"One can choose to go back toward safety or forward toward growth. Growth must be chosen again and again; fear must be overcome again and again."

- Abraham Maslow

Chapter 1
ALISON

The chilly wind of the autumn afternoon shook the window in Abby's studio. Alison shivered, pulling her half-naked body a little closer to Victoria as Abby fiddled with the settings on her camera. Sliding her fingers under the edge of the deep red satin panties, Alison gave them a small tug, ensuring they smoothly followed the curve of her butt.

"Abby, darling, I know you want to pay for the renovations yourself, but please at least let me pay to have heating installed. If you work in here over the winter, you'll freeze to death. Or if you don't, your clients will." Victoria wrapped her arms around Alison, pulling them closer still. The three of them, Victoria, Abby, and Alison, had been at this photo shoot business for over three hours already and while Abby was still brimming with enthusiasm, Alison was growing a little weary.

When the *Darkness* article showcasing their highly specialised Airbnb (a property which catered for those with a slight kink) had landed, they'd all been so excited. The magazine had given the place a full four-page spread, and the images were nothing short of breathtaking, almost as breathtaking as the volume of bookings that had followed. Except for four consecutive days in December, they had bookings for the property covering the next eight months. Even the two notoriously toughest weeks in the tourism industry—the third week in January and the second week in February— were gone, and at full price. They couldn't have asked for more, and that's what Victoria had told Bryce, her long-term friend and the publication's editor, when she called to thank him.

But Bryce was always on the lookout for his next feature, and he wasn't shy or slow in requesting payback for their gratitude when Victoria had told him about their little ménage à trois now that Alison was fully back in Victoria (and Abby's) life.

"I can see it now. A Christmas feature of Victoria, the saintly domme and her two elf subs," he had teased as all three of them had gathered around the speaker, listening in to the call. But he hadn't been teasing. In fact, when he had offered them a free advertising package for their adult retail business in exchange for the feature, the offer became serious.

While Victoria wasn't one for exposing herself so publicly, Alison knew she was also a shrewd businesswoman. *Darkness* was by far the most popular magazine publication of its kind in Europe and had a rapidly growing audience in North America.

"I'd want the piece to feature and promote Alison's furniture, the tantra chairs and such, and I want Abby to do the shoot."

Bryce had been understandably nervous about the shoot being orchestrated by one of the subjects, but Alison had listened as Victoria assured him that not only was Abby one of the most talented photographers she had ever known, refusing to hire her would be a deal breaker. After initial objections, reluctantly, he'd agreed. Alison had to chuckle to herself because she knew that one of Victoria's silent motivations for insisting Abby do the shoot was that her mistress wouldn't have been relaxed enough to even contemplate such a thing with a complete stranger. For all of Victoria's outward confidence and bravado, Alison knew Victoria had a shy streak and the entire experience would be well out of her comfort zone.

So here they were, dressed in scanty outfits of provocatively festive ruby reds and emerald greens around a Christmas tree in the middle of a cold October afternoon.

After the roaring success of the piece Bryce had written, he had been desperate to do a follow-up piece on its owners. Bryce had been beside himself when he found out that Victoria didn't just have one sub but two, telling them that this was exactly what his readers wanted to see. So that was why, on an overcast October afternoon, all three of them were semi-naked; Alison draped over a chaise longue with Victoria by her side, as Abby adjusted the lights, and set the timer on her Nikon, before running into the position for the shot. Alison lifted her leg, wrapping it over Abby's limb as Victoria stood above them, brandishing a leather crop.

"Okay, positions, please!" Abby declared, brandishing the remote shutter in her hand.

Alison lay on the chaise longue on her side, lifting her leg to allow Abby to slot in underneath her as they had rehearsed earlier, and Victoria stood in a wide stance above them, brandishing a serious-looking crop.

"Hold still and smoulder!" Abby tilted her head up a little towards the camera, and with a movement so quick Alison couldn't see it, she snapped the shutter into life and it illuminated the room in a sudden flash. "Just another couple to make sure," she said with authority. Several bursts of harsh light later and Alison's vision faded to bright white.

"Abby, is this the last shot? It's so cold here that if we don't heat Alison soon, I'm afraid she'll become hypothermic. She has an icicle hanging from her nose." Victoria wrapped her arms around her body again in what seemed to be a desperate attempt to hold on to the last of her warmth. Not that there would be much of that left now.

"I've just got one more shot I'd like to do." Abby jumped up from the chaise longue, almost knocking Alison flying.

Alison rolled her eyes at Victoria and let out an enormous sigh. Abby was a perfectionist. There was no doubt from what they'd already seen the images would be stunning, but Alison and Victoria were becoming a little weary.

"Alison, can you get into position against the cross, please?"

Alison glanced over at Victoria, raising an eyebrow in question, but Victoria just gave a slight shrug. Evidently, she was as much in the dark as Alison. But she did as she was told, leaning her weight against the polished oak. With nimble fingers, Abby secured both her wrists and ankles in place and, much to Alison's surprise, covered her eyes with a thick velvet blindfold. Suddenly, this shoot was becoming more interesting.

Alison took in a deep breath, fully expecting to be left standing in that position for at least the next ten minutes while Abby organised Victoria and then got herself sorted. Alison rolled her eyes under the mask. She'd have no idea how this scene would look until she saw the finished image.

"I want you to warm me up when I get into position and then use the crop. I've set the cameras up to run, so they will just take continual bursts. It means we can forget about them and let them work away." Abby's voice was so authoritative it almost made Alison giggle. But it wasn't laughter that was on her mind when she felt the warmth of Abby's body against her own. In fact, it was her gasp that filled the air when Abby's fingertips worked their way down her body. What was she doing? Where was she going? Alison knew what she wanted the answer to be…and sure enough as Abby reached the ruby-coloured satin panties which Alison was wearing, the pressure against her centre increased, followed by a popping noise as she ripped open the two studs holding the crotch in place. A thrill of excitement shot through Alison's body. The room had suddenly become much hotter.

"Maybe I should gag you too?" Abby whispered playfully as she allowed two long fingers to slide between Alison's lips. The musky scent that Abby was wearing filled her senses. God, that felt good.

"Ahem." Victoria cleared her throat. "You know your mistress is still standing here…watching you?"

Alison felt the loss as Abby quickly pulled her hand away. *Never mind*, she thought, *I'll get my own back on her later.*

"Sorry, Mistress." Abby's voice sounded demure and even though Alison couldn't see her, she knew the younger woman had her head bowed. "If you can stand just here and bend that way slightly when you touch me and then whip me?" Abby's voice was almost a question with inflection. That authoritative edge had gone. It was incredible the way the power dynamic changed with just a few words and a position change.

The sound of shuffling coming from in front of her let Alison know Abby was close, but she didn't appreciate how close until she felt her breath tickle her swollen clit. *Oh, my.*

Alison tried to imagine the unseen scene unfolding in front of her. Abby was on her knees. Victoria had a crop in her hands. Abby had mentioned it earlier, but equally she could hear the dull thump of the leather against what she thought was probably her mistress's palm as she patiently waited for Abby to tell her when to start.

"If you could just whip me, Mistress? Please?"

Alison braced herself as she felt Abby's mouth close in on her centre. First it tickled just a little, then as her tongue slid into the start of her wetness, a tingle spread across her centre and down over her thighs. Abby's tongue was masterful and she let out an appreciative groan.

As other noises filled the air, Alison was vaguely aware of them, but she had neither the inclination nor the ability to pull her attention away from the way Abby's mouth was toying with her. A long groan escaped her chest as Abby's flattened tongue slowly made its way over her centre; it was languid and sensual. Her legs shook. With the small amount of movement she could muster, Alison pushed her hips forward, desperately wanting more of Abby's mouth.

"Oh, that feels g-ood." Alison's voice hitched as slow strokes moved to firm flicks over her clit.

The crack of a crop landing on soft flesh made both women jolt. The hot exhalation from Abby's mouth made Alison moan again before she could stifle it.

"Did I say you could talk?" Victoria's voice had a deeper, sexy edge, and Alison immediately knew her mistress was fully engaged in this shot. Equally, there was something thrilling about hearing Abby being chastised. Over the last few months of therapy, Alison had been aware of the change within her. It was subtle at first, and she dismissed it. But over the last few weeks, as she'd felt stronger, she was suddenly aware of the thrill of power when she got close to Abby.

The crack of the crop cut through the air without warning. Alison took a sharp breath. Even though she felt no pain, there was an exhilaration at hearing Abby's gasp. The corners of her mouth turned up into a small smile as she imagined the red line which would appear against Abby's porcelain skin. But she had little time to smile. Abby sucked her in, moving slowly at first and then faster.

Alison let her head fall back, losing herself in the delicious sensation in her centre and the crack of the crop as it made contact with her lover at the hand of her mistress. The intensity of the tingle rose from the soles of her feet upwards. "I'm going to come." It was more of a statement than a request, something else that had been changing over the last few weeks.

The sound of the crop lit the air once again.

"I want you to make Kitten come harder than she's ever done before, my Pet. Can you do that for me?"

Alison felt Abby's tongue slide up and down over her clit as she confirmed she'd do as her mistress had instructed. The intensity and roughness of her movement stepped up in tempo until Alison screamed, shaking, losing control. Her orgasm ripped through her body, pulling her restraints tight against her wrists and ankles as her body spasmed, but still Abby didn't stop.

Again, the rush of euphoria swept through her body, leaving her gasping for breath.

"Enough, please. I need you to stop," she begged.

"Well done, my Pet."

Alison sagged in her restraints, wetness trickling down the inside of her thigh.

"It's time for me to hold you both." Victoria pulled the blindfold from Alison's eyes.

Squinting in the sudden brightness, she was grateful as her mistress undid the cuffs around her wrists and ankles. Victoria laid her down next to Abby, then joined them both. Alison watched as their mistress ran a soothing hand across the younger woman's red buttocks.

Uninvited, Alison joined her mistress, running her

fingertips over Abby's tender flesh, all the while trying to rein in her urge to slide her hand between the young woman's legs. To do that, she'd have to wait for her mistress's permission, something which was becoming increasingly frustrating.

Chapter 2
ALISON

Alison twisted around in her chair towards the open fire, holding up her palms towards the orange glow. Braw Coories was becoming a regular Sunday lunch haunt for the three of them, but today wasn't a Sunday, it was a Wednesday and the usual weekend punters in their woolly jumpers and bobble hats were replaced by office types in smart suits. What else would you expect on a weekday in the heart of Edinburgh's Old Town? They were only a ten minute stroll from the parliament building which, to Alison, explained the dour expressions of the work-weary patrons all wishing it was Friday instead of hump day.

It was the Gothic decor that Alison loved as it gave the place a sense of the dramatic. Victoria enjoyed their visits here for the quality of their wine menu, but for Abby, the choice was much simpler; they did an *awesome* fish finger sandwich and dirty fries with the added bonus of Noble Isle hand wash and moisturiser in the loo. No wonder Victoria loved her so much. She was an unpretentious free spirit who knew what she liked and never apologised for being herself.

Much of that growing confidence had emerged since she

had been with Victoria. Gone was the shy, almost nervous young woman that she and Mhairi had met at the house in Aberdour all those months ago. *God, had it really only been a matter of months? Surely it must be longer?*

Alison marvelled at the way human connections worked. There were some people you could have known for years, some more intimately than others, whether via work, sports, or, god help you, a relationship, yet the roots you'd established were nothing more than superficial. Like a silver maple planted in sandy soil. Everything looks great until along comes Nelly, a Category 1 storm with gusts of over a hundred miles per hour. Before you know it, the landscape has changed beyond all recognition. As though Hollywood swept in with a disaster movie. And yet, in stark contrast, there were relationships like this: the bond between her and Abby. They'd only known each other for months, and yet it felt so much longer. It was as though they could reach inside each other and touch the hidden parts of what made them who they were. Alison almost giggled as she realised that was both literal, and metaphorical. But what they shared wasn't the same as the tie that held Victoria and Abby together, or the one that held her and Victoria together.

Victoria was her constant. The refuge against the world when life tried to rip her apart. But just like a safe harbour, it isn't where you want to berth your yacht all year round. Alison leant back in her chair, musing about her choice of analogies. She blamed her therapist, who encouraged her to use them to access her emotions. *It'll help you understand and explain them*, she'd told Alison. In her sessions with Olivia, or Dr Olivia Hopkins, as she preferred to be called, analogies were now commonplace. Why talk about the importance of personal growth and moving on from relationships when you could talk about flamingos and the salt flats of Bolivia? Because just like them, Alison had to move on with her life.

The natural world documentary seemed like such an innocuous choice for a wet autumn evening, but when she'd seen the chicks trapped in restraints of solidified salt, crying for their mothers, she'd been in floods of tears. Keep moving or else you'll die. That was one hell of an analogy.

Sitting next to the roaring fire listening to Victoria and Abby's chatter, she was glad she'd moved on from Mhairi, albeit she had the slightest pang of sadness. That melancholy wasn't because she missed Mhairi, good lord no, but watching how Abby and Victoria looked at each other brought home the fact she was missing...something.

No doubt it would be the primary topic of conversation with Olivia this afternoon. The woman always made it sound as though it was her that was directing the sessions, even starting by asking Alison, "So, what do you want to talk about today?" But then, before Alison knew what had happened, they were wading through a thick treacle of emotions which Alison had buried under layers (and years) of avoidance. Olivia saw through her tricks—like inserting humour to dodge pain, or pulling Alison back as she swerved sharply to the left to avoid the emotional obstacle that stood in her path.

Olivia took her hand, encouraging her to face what lay ahead. To dismantle it, piece by piece, in her own time until she could see a way through. A small shiver ran through Alison's body as she imagined Olivia bowing her head just a little so she could peer over the rim of her glasses. The woman was so damned sexy! There was something so very prim about her, in looks at least, as she sat in her low cross-cut dress that sat just above the knee. The material was a dark silk overlaid with the most beautiful embroidered flowers and Alison had memorised every inch of its pattern and the legs that it barely covered as she crossed and uncrossed her legs.

They call it transference.

Transference: /ˈtransf(ə)r(ə)ns,ˈtrɑːnsf(ə)r(ə)ns, ˈtranzf(ə)r(ə)ns,ˈtrɑːnzf(ə)r(ə)ns/

noun: transference neurosis

A redirection of feelings from someone else to your therapist, often in the form of romantic emotions.

Alison absently ran her fingers along the length of her knife, lost in thought, as she waited for her meal to arrive. Was what she was feeling transference? She didn't think so, but probably every patient (or client, as the profession now liked to call them) thought the same. And then there was the counter-transference vibes she was getting from Olivia. Their conversations stimulated the therapist, Alison was sure of that. It was little things, like the way Olivia wriggled in her seat when Alison talked about her sexual preferences.

"Ground control to Alison." Victoria's voice snapped Alison back to attention. There was a flush on her cheeks which hadn't come from the heat of the fire. Giving a tight smile, she was aware of an odd niggle of guilt in her stomach. Here she was with two women who loved her, and her them, but she was having fantasies about her therapist. She didn't deserve them.

"Sorry, I was miles away."

"What time is your appointment?" Victoria lifted her napkin, and shook out the folds before placing it over her lap.

"Three," Alison offered but didn't elaborate and Victoria simply nodded, understanding that the conversation wasn't going any further, today at least.

But Alison rarely talked about her therapy sessions, choosing instead to process internally. It had been hard for the first while, with two or three sessions in a single week, but now they'd gone to once a week. Alison knew she was one of the lucky ones. Not only had she got out (with the help of friends) but she'd had the financial resources and contacts to put herself straight into therapy, something which was proving to be equally as painful as it was rewarding. She was on the cusp of diverting the conversation when the waitress appeared, brandishing plates.

"Fish finger sandwich?"

Abby raised her hand and smiled at the young redhead, but Alison didn't miss the way Victoria's hand squeezed her other lover's knee, raising an eyebrow as their gazes met.

That was what Alison wanted.

Chapter 3
ALISON

"So, what do you want to talk about today?"

Alison allowed herself a small smile and pushed back against the soft plum-coloured cushions on the sofa. Tucking her feet underneath where she sat, she thought for a moment. What did she want to start with? How stunning Olivia looked in the cream daisy print dress? Or would she compliment the way her strawberry blonde waves so delicately kissed the soft skin of her neck? Catching herself, she knew what she should talk about—this whole transference thing, but that wasn't what she said. Rather, she opted for much safer ground.

"I'm not sure how long term my current relationship is going to last." There, she'd said it. The words that had been gnawing away inside had finally made it past her lips and were now living in the real world. Even scarier was the fact she hadn't been the only one to hear them.

"What makes you say that?" Olivia uncrossed her legs and leant forward, cocking her head in curiosity.

It's not because I have any romantic feelings towards you,

Alison scolded herself silently, before then thinking how beautiful her therapist was looking today.

"It's not that I don't love them, I do, and I'm really grateful to them for—well—everything." Alison paused for a moment, tipping her head back to stare at the large bookcases that lined the opposite wall while she searched for the words. "I want what they've got."

It was true she wanted somebody to look at her the way Abby looked at Victoria, just as they had done over lunch. The same intimate glances the two of them shared while all three of them made love.

"And what's that?" Olivia asked, but Alison stared back at her with a blank expression. She hadn't heard her question because she was lost in her own thoughts. "What do they have that you want?" Olivia asked again, but more pointedly this time.

"I want their bond. I want my own Victoria." Alison faltered just for a moment. Was it Victoria she wanted?

"Tell me what went through your head right there." Olivia narrowed her eyes and pointed the top of her silver pen at Alison.

Shit. Alison hated when she did this. The tiniest bit of leakage and the woman went into full-blown therapy mode, crawling all over it like a wasp on an iced bun.

"I was just thinking about how much I wanted what they have." She shrugged to divert Olivia from trying to excavate the current hole she'd dug herself into.

"But you had Victoria before? And now you're saying you want her again? To yourself?"

Alison shook her head, but the way Olivia looked at her suggested the therapist didn't believe she was being offered a full and frank disclosure. One more quick diversion and Alison could clamber back up the crater on to firmer ground.

"No. I mean, I want somebody to feel about me the way

she feels about Abby, and Abby feels about her. But I don't want to split them up. They're made for each other. I just want to have that connection, too, but with someone else… my own person."

What Alison didn't add on to the end of her statement was, *someone like you.*

"So, you feel confident if you went into another relationship—a one-on-one with someone new—that you wouldn't recreate the issues you experienced with Mhairi? Is that what you're telling me?"

Alison nodded.

"And how do you know that wouldn't happen again? How did it happen the first time?"

Alison shrugged. She knew the answer. In part, it was because she desperately wanted to push boundaries. She wanted the high of the next new thing. Part through greed, part through maturity, and part through the exhilaration of being able to get more. When she first met Mhairi, she was like a kid in the sweet shop. Gone were the restraints that Victoria had placed on her. Suddenly she was with a woman who would give her anything and everything, and sometimes more than she wanted. With a decent domme, it would never have gotten that far, but with a partner as toxic as Mhairi, well, they fed each other's base needs.

"You've gone somewhere in your head," Olivia said.

"I was just thinking what a destructive match Mhairi and I were."

Olivia nodded. "Do you think if Mhairi had been with someone else, that she would have turned out differently, too?" Olivia asked. "What about her last subs? Did she treat them any differently to the way she treated you?"

Alison knew what Olivia was doing. This wasn't her fault, none of this was her fault. But still, there was a little niggle in the pit of her stomach that worried her. Perhaps she had unleashed something in Mhairi. She had somehow set the scene for everything that had come afterwards. "I just think sometimes you meet somebody who brings out the worst in you, and I think we brought out the worst in each other. But no, Mhairi will always be Mhairi. Maybe I just got her there faster."

"But you said when this all first started, you had a choice. Didn't Mhairi, too, have a choice?" Alison nodded. "And what do you feel happened to that choice as the relationship went on?"

Alison thought for a moment. "I suppose I didn't always feel like I had a choice. I know it sounds stupid to say it now, but she told me it was what I wanted, what I needed. And when somebody tells you that often enough, then…you believe them. Especially when they keep telling you with everything else in your life that you're wrong or not good enough, that they know what's right for you." She paused for a second, looking down at her feet. God, now she was out of that relationship, she couldn't believe how stupid she'd been. Glancing back up at Olivia, she said, "she told me no one else would understand me. That I was depraved." She snorted. "That the only person who *got me* was her; she knew what I needed, and I just believed her. And she was so cutting about Victoria. Somewhere along the line, it all got warped. I've spoken to Victoria about it since, like recently, and for years, Mhairi had me believing it was Victoria who didn't want me. But that wasn't the case. It was really me who left Victoria. For years she thought she wasn't enough for me. It all got so twisted."

"How did you feel when Victoria told you that?" Olivia asked.

"Guilty. I didn't realise I had what I had, when I had it."

"But you have her back now, and yet you want something more." Olivia cocked her head, raising her eyebrows, waiting for Alison to say more.

But Alison just laughed. It was ridiculous. When said like that, it really was ridiculous. Here she was, regretting having lost Victoria all those years ago, for not appreciating her mistress, relieved and happy to have her back, along with Abby, but she still wanted more.

"I love Victoria deeply and she's shown me that the intensity of love that I want is real. I watch her and Abby and they have it, and you can have that without giving away your self-respect. They have something different, something deeper and I…it's something I don't share in. I can't. Not with them. The way they look at each other, the way they look into each other's eyes." Alison looked up, trying to read Olivia's face. Did she understand what she meant? Their eyes met and Olivia stared intently at her as if she could see straight into Alison's soul.

"Tell me what that feels like?" asked Olivia. The two of them didn't take their eyes off each other.

"It feels like the world will stop spinning if that person isn't in your life anymore. It feels like they know what you're thinking or feeling without you having to say a word."

Surely she must feel this too, Alison thought, but Olivia appeared to be giving nothing away, so Alison opted to move to safer ground: talking about Victoria and Abby.

"They have this way of speaking without saying a word. One look and there's this flash of telepathy. Sometimes it's small things, like Abby seems to know when Victoria needs a glass of wine or even a cup of tea. Before you say anything, it's not because she has them at set times."

Olivia held her palms up in defence as though she hadn't been about to say anything of the sort, but Alison ignored her, ploughing on.

"Nothing is routine about Victoria. But Abby can just sense when she needs something. It's even like that in bed. I mean, we're both devoted to Victoria, but it runs deeper with them. Victoria knows Abby's body so well she can keep her on the edge of orgasm for hours, long after I've come, gone and got the t-shirt."

Alison rolled her eyes, then suddenly realised how what she'd been saying had piqued her therapist's interest. Olivia's eyes were a little wider. Her quick moving pen had slowed, breaking contact with the page as though the small strokes she made with her hand had the ink toying with the paper.

"Go on," Olivia said, moving her pen as if to usher Alison to reveal more.

Alison wasn't about to let this opportunity pass her by, not when she could have so much fun.

"The other night, we'd been in my studio, Victoria and I, and I wanted to try out these new stocks I've designed, so we shouted Abby through. She has the building next to mine and there's this corridor thing that links the two. Anyway," Alison waved her hands, "that's not important. To test them, Victoria wanted me bent over and secured in place. It's sort of like…" Alison rose from the sofa, throwing the cushion she'd been cradling aside and bent over so she was side-on to Olivia. "My hands are secured here, my head here, and my feet,"—she widened her stance—"here. I designed it with a spacer bar for the feet. Wide enough to keep the sub open. Or in this case, me. So I need you to imagine me naked, bound and wide open." Alison shoogled her booty a little, glancing over to Olivia to make sure she was still listening.

The therapist seemed enrapt by Alison's description, her mouth hanging open. Alison smiled, not missing a beat.

"Well, Victoria tells Abby, who's now also naked apart from this huge strap-on, that she wants her to make me come but to take it slowly…like excruciatingly slowly, so that I have to beg. Victoria loves it when I beg. Now, after she said that, they didn't speak again, and Abby set to work. She teased me senseless, I had her fingers rubbing my clit and deep inside me, then she slipped her tongue into my butt until I was pulling against the restraints, screaming for her to use the strap-on." Alison's arms and fingers flew around her body showing how Abby had got her into such a state, all the while out the corner of her eye watching Olivia squirm. "And then I glimpsed them. There's a mirror in the corner of the room, and even in the state I was in—I mean, I can't remember ever being so desperate to be fucked—I saw them. Abby was doing exactly what Victoria wanted, just through a series of quick glances. They're so attuned to each other."

"And did she…?" Olivia swallowed hard, her eyes locked on Alison.

"Did she what?" Alison asked demurely.

"Fuck you. Did she fuck you?" Olivia's voice hitched, and she uncrossed her legs and then crossed them again the other way. Alison smiled, then sat back down on the sofa, keeping her legs apart.

"She did. Hard and deep, just like Victoria wanted her to." Alison ran her hands down the front of her thighs, amused by what she thought was her therapist's obvious arousal.

Olivia nodded, biting down on her bottom lip. "Have you considered the reason it worked isn't just because they know each other so well, but they know you, too?"

"What?" Alison wasn't sure what sort of reply she expected from the woman, but suggesting that she might already be in the right relationship wasn't the option she'd have selected from the supper menu. A sense of dejection threatened to swallow her whole.

"As you were the one they were both focussing their attention on pleasuring, directly or indirectly, and were so obviously successful in doing so, it seems reasonable to conclude the bond isn't just between the two of them but you too." Olivia let her words land and seemed comfortable with the silence that followed. Alison said nothing.

"But you don't see it that way, and that is far more interesting. Don't you agree?" Olivia said eventually. Alison did not agree.

Chapter 4
DR OLIVIA HOPKINS

Olivia sat at the second table in the window area of Greens of George Street, an old-fashioned brasserie. She'd been nursing the medium skinny coconut latte, with an extra shot, for well over an hour now, painfully aware of the waiter's glances in her direction as the place filled up with office workers arriving sharply to secure themselves a table for lunch. She checked her watch, it was 11.50. If she wasn't careful, they would physically eject her and her everlasting coffee, and replace her with a Soup of the Day or Haddock Fishcake. In any other circumstances, she'd either order lunch or leave, allowing somebody else to get the table. But the seat offered a perfect viewing point for the grand glass-fronted office building opposite. From here she could see straight into the marble reception area, seeing everyone who came, and more importantly, went from the building.

When Olivia had checked the directory, it seemed to be home to two of the city's more prominent law firms. At 10:30, she had followed the woman as she approached the tall glass doors with the stride of a woman with purpose. Certainly far more purpose than Olivia had this morning.

Even as the redhead made her way to the elevators, nodding to the chap on reception, she seemed to give out the air of someone who was exactly where they were meant to be in that moment.

Olivia checked her watch again. 11:55. A draught blew around her ankles as the door to the coffee house opened again, admitting even more hungry, hopeful patrons. No wonder they wanted the table. But she couldn't leave. If she left now, where would she go? Loitering outside on the pavement would look suspicious, so that wasn't an option. Attracting the waiter's attention, she ordered a simple black tea. He took her order and continued to wait. It was another ten elongated seconds before Olivia realised he expected her to order food as well. *Hell, could he make this any more painful than it already was?*

"That's all, thanks," she said with an apologetic smile.

He rolled his eyes and gave a small but audible *tut*. Perhaps she should have ordered panini too, but she couldn't order another coffee, that was for sure. Normally a one-coffee-a-day-girl, she'd broken all of her rules and already had three so far, leaving her wired to the moon. The thought brought a chuckle. It had been a saying she'd always loved, *wired to the moon*. When she'd first qualified as a psychotherapist, her work in some of the rougher areas of Glasgow brought her into contact with addicts, most of whom had used that saying, rather than just saying they were high. Surely she too must be high on something to be sitting here stalking a stranger, because no one of sound mind would consider her current actions to be reasonable…for a therapist. Even now, she could internally rationalise the recent choices she'd been making.

Shaking the thoughts from her head, she doubled her efforts to focus on the building across the street. So intense was her gaze that she almost didn't realise the waiter had come back with her order until he was upon her. Jumping in fright, she caused the chap to spill a little of the amber liquid from the small silver teapot onto the tray.

"Oh. Sorry. I didn't see you there."

"Evidently." Another roll of his eyes followed. Olivia gave him a tight smile and bit back a more pointed retort. She couldn't afford to engage with him just now or she might miss her leaving.

"I'll pay for it now, if you don't mind," she said, her gaze returning towards the window. Her actions were rude, but she didn't care. This was more important than his feelings and hadn't he already been so rude to her? A quick glance at his expression suggested he did mind.

"Just pay for it when you leave."

"No, no, I want to pay for it now."

He let out an exasperated sigh, then thankfully left to get the payment terminal.

If the woman appeared, Olivia needed to be ready to follow, and having to queue in line during a lunch hour rush to pay for a coconut latte and black tea would scupper her plans. No, she'd enable herself to burst into action at a moment's notice—although that moment didn't look like it was happening soon.

As she sat and waited, she thought back to Alison's last session…her client's session. The woman was teasing her, and Olivia knew it. But it did something to her. Something she couldn't articulate, and since their last meeting, she'd become borderline obsessive thinking about Alison. The way she looked at her. The way she sat. The way her mouth just tugged up at the corners when she smiled. This was something completely new for Olivia, something completely out of her comfort zone. Technically, Olivia should have recused herself as Alison's therapist, but the idea of losing contact with her? Well, that was something she wasn't ready to do.

Even when she came up with this madcap idea of just getting to know them a bit better, she knew she was crossing boundaries. Olivia didn't cross boundaries…until now. But there was something intriguing about the relationship that Alison described, which made Olivia want to know more. *This will help me understand her better,* she'd told herself. It was patient research. Perhaps not the most conventional research, but it was driven by professional intent…wasn't it?

There were so many times that she could have turned away, like this morning when she sat in her car at the end of the estate driveway, waiting for the Defender to appear. But she hadn't. Instead, she'd followed the vehicle as it weaved its way through traffic into the city centre. Her little electric Volkswagen ID.5, which was very planet-conscious, seemed tiny compared to the distinctive 4x4 she was following, but at least she was reassuringly inconspicuous.

The waiter appeared with the terminal, thrusting it towards her. As she placed her card against it, hearing the beep of an approved payment, she noticed movement from across the street. The redhead was on the move. Victoria had left the building.

"Thank you." Withdrawing her card and lifting her bag in one easy movement, Olivia rose from the table. Pulling out a pair of sunglasses, she made for the door, leaving the waiter in her wake.

"The tip?" he called after her.

"I don't think so," she said, rolling her eyes before sliding on her sunglasses.

Chapter 5
ALISON

Alison pushed open the heavy door of the farmhouse, letting her bag drop at her feet. It made a soft thud against the cold flagstone floor. The day had been long, filled with client meetings; a couple in Edinburgh, followed by a longer final meeting just outside Hermitage, in the borders, which had drained the last of her reserves. It was her bed she'd been thinking about for the entire long two-hour drive back. But not before a glass of wine.

Grabbing a glass from the kitchen cabinet, she poured herself a generous measure from the already open bottle of Barossa Shiraz Victoria had left on the side. Leaning against the counter she drank, swirling it around her mouth before swallowing. The fullness of its body seemed to coat her insides with warmth, allowing her shoulders to drop as she let go of tension. *God, this is good stuff*, she thought, reaching for the bottle and topping up her glass again. It probably wasn't a good idea to drink on an empty stomach, but she wasn't in the mood to cook, and the idea of cheese and crackers was less than inspiring.

Too tired to watch TV or read, she headed upstairs. The

house was so quiet Alison assumed that Victoria and Abby had gone out for dinner. That was one of the wonderful things about the renovation. They got to live in a period home, but without a single creak from the old floorboards or a groan from an antiquated heating system. Instead, the internal structure had been renovated sympathetically around the original features, all of which they'd kept.

While, more often than not, the three of them slept in the one bed, Victoria had been adamant they all had their own space. So they each had a bedroom and then there was the room they all shared. But that wasn't where Alison wanted to go tonight, not when the safety and sanctuary of her own room was beckoning. She and Abby were different. Abby would have been happy to be in Victoria's company 24/7, whereas Alison...she treasured her time on her own. She liked her own company, and after a long hard day like the one she'd had today, that's all she wanted—her own company.

A creak, followed by a rustle of movement, was the first indication she wasn't alone. Alison froze to the spot at the top of the stairs. Listening. The alarm hadn't been armed when she'd entered the house...that was unusual. A spike of adrenaline shot through her system and she was suddenly aware of the rushing of blood in her ears. *Please, god, don't let it be Mhairi.* She held her breath. The noises seemed to come from their shared room. There was a groan and then the unmistakable sound of a giggle.

Alison exhaled, relieved to realise the giggle was Abby's. Rolling her eyes, she crept across the landing, not wanting to disturb them. If she hadn't been so tired, she might have changed and gone to join them, but not tonight. The last meeting of the day had been boring, or at least it was until they had reached the basement and the clients announced they'd like her to design them a dungeon. Thankfully, she'd stifled a laugh when they announced their request. Both in their sixties, with an aura of 'retired dentist', she couldn't imagine two people who looked less likely to have a dungeon.

He'd been something big in insurance but now retired, and she…Alison had a vague memory of her wittering on about charitable work—yes, that was it, *re-homing designer clothes*. What a worthy cause. Not. Alison had studied them, trying to work out who was the dominant, and who was the submissive, although she struggled to imagine either of them in skin tight latex…thankfully. But that was the thing about their lifestyle, you couldn't always tell who was who until you saw them in action.

The door was ajar, and she saw the silhouette of Abby's naked body moving above Victoria. Their moans were increasing in both volume and frequency. For a moment, she thought about going in and sitting on the small red chair by the window to watch as she sipped her wine—Abby always liked it when she watched—but decided against it.

Stripping off the constraints of her clothes, she slid beneath the duvet and listened to them make love. Her hand snaked its way down her stomach to the arousal which was piquing between her legs. Her fingers slid deftly through her wetness, determined to catch up with the action she was hearing. Every whimper and groan brought her closer to orgasm until Abby screamed.

"Please. Please, let me come. Mistress, I'm desperate to come—please."

Victoria's voice was stern when she replied. "Not until I tell you." And then there was a crack. Alison imagined it might be the crop which Abby was so fond of. She imagined it hitting the young woman's porcelain skin. A shudder of arousal crashed through her body. The idea of being the one to wield the crop was awakening something in her which she hadn't even known was there. It was unlike anything she'd experienced before. With the background noise of Abby's begging *please, please Mistress, let me come*, she brought herself to orgasm, harder than she'd ever done alone, and in perfect synchronisation with Abby. Matching Abby's timing had happened before, but certainly not whilst they were in different rooms.

Panting, she tried to catch her breath, quite overcome by what had just happened. Part of her wanted to go through and join them, to share in the post-coital glow, but she didn't. For several minutes, the house fell silent, as though it, too, was recovering from the tremors. Then she heard soft muffled voices. Alison wasn't really listening, but then she heard her name. Her ears perked up. She rose from the bed and walked towards the doors. The farmhouse was old, with thick walls, but the doors to the rooms were ajar. Silently, she stepped out into the hall. This wasn't a conversation between domme and sub, it was Victoria and Abby talking. Again, she heard her name being mentioned.

Eavesdropping was an awful thing to do, but she had an unexplainable urge to hear what was being said.

"I can't help it. It's guilt, I suppose," Abby said, leaving Alison wondering what on earth the young woman had to feel guilty about.

"What we have is different," she heard Victoria say. She leaned in closer. "Nothing will ever break the connection between you and me. It runs deeper. Nobody expects you to have the same depth of feelings for Alison," Victoria assured the younger woman.

Abby gave a murmured assent. *Abby was feeling guilty because she didn't love her? Was that it?*

"But that doesn't mean I don't miss her when she's not here, or wish she could have been here tonight." Abby's voice had the slightest tinge of pain, and Alison wanted to soothe her. Instead, she stood on the landing, holding her breath, listening.

"Understand that with Alison, everything is changing. She's healing, and as she heals, she'll become stronger. You never know, she might want different things. She may want more than we can give her, and we have to be prepared for that."

Alison couldn't help wondering if Victoria was worried about history repeating itself. After all, she had already left Victoria once because she'd wanted more, more than her mistress could give her. *But that wasn't the case now, was it?*

Victoria spoke again. Alison held her breath, waiting to hear what would come next. "No matter what she decides, she'll always have a place in our lives. But don't set your expectations too high, at least not until she figures it out for herself."

The bed creaked, freezing Alison to the spot. Someone was getting up. The fear of being found eavesdropping forced her into action, quickly retreating to her room. She didn't want them to know what she'd heard. *Was it true? Did life hold different things for her?* She wasn't sure, but strangely, the idea didn't upset her, although she couldn't articulate why. Perhaps as she healed, she would want different things. But it was far too soon to make those types of decisions.

Chapter 6
ALISON

The roads were slick with rain; they almost shimmered in the soft sun of the autumn morning. Gold, coppers, and russets of leaves, more on the ground than there were in the trees, gave a warm hue to the day. Victoria was driving, Alison sat next to her and Abby was in the back, editing. She had been at a Halloween event the night before, a LGBTQIA+ charity do, and had promised to get the shots over within twenty-four hours. No mean feat considering she didn't get back until 3 a.m. But Abby was nothing if not dutiful. When she made a promise, she stuck to it. Alison turned in her seat, watching her edit furiously, fingers moving at lightning speed. Ed Sheeran played on the radio. Perfect. And Alison wondered, *is this perfect?*

Ever since she had overheard Victoria and Abby's conversation, she'd been questioning the reliability and stability of her happiness, giving the subject far more thought than was probably healthy. Could she be happy with exactly what she had? Would that yearning for a special bond she'd talked about with Olivia fade away? If it didn't, was she ungrateful for wanting more than she had? She wasn't sure.

The only thing she was sure of was that she didn't want to break away from the two people she was closest to…that she loved. This was the nearest she'd ever come to any form of contentment. But when she saw Abby and Victoria look at each other, she saw something she didn't have, and inside she had a growing need to have that connection with someone of her own. She turned her gaze towards Victoria, whose face was very serious, noticing she kept glancing in her rearview mirror. Not once, or twice, but several times.

Alison turned in her seat, trying to look out to the road behind, but the headrests in the Defender's backseat meant that she couldn't get a clear view. Turning to the side mirror, she bent forward, angling herself so she could see what was holding Victoria's attention. She'd half expected to see a teenager in a pimped Fiesta, driving too close, because that would explain the constant glancing in the mirror, but all she could see was a small blue car which seemed to be a reasonable distance away.

"What are you doing?" Victoria asked her.

"I'm just trying to see what you're looking at. You keep looking in your mirror and I'm curious."

Victoria shrugged. "Oh, it's nothing. You don't need to worry about it."

"Are you sure?" Alison asked.

"No, honestly, it's…it's, umm…it's nothing."

The grave expression which was etched across Victoria's face didn't suggest 'it was nothing' to Alison, and as they turned off the main road onto the quiet single track that led to the house in Aberdour, Alison ducked down and squinted in the side mirror. The blue car turned into the road behind them. Even Alison shivered against the warmth of the heated seat.

"That's not what your face says." Alison watched as Victoria grimaced.

"Honestly, I'm just being paranoid. Ignore me."

"Paranoid?" Alison said. "You? You're the last person who'd ever be paranoid."

Victoria shrugged again. "I know. It's just that...well... when I nipped into town the other day to see the lawyer, I had this weird feeling I was being followed, but when I stopped and looked around, I couldn't see anyone. Or I couldn't see anyone who appeared to be interested in me. You're going to think I'm stupid. I am stupid, because it's my imagination playing tricks on me. I know that."

"Well, there must be *something* if it's bothering you this much," said Alison.

"Mm. I was walking along George Street, on my way to see Callie to drop in some new designs. Her new tailor shop is on Rose Street—it's gorgeous, by the way—and I swear it felt like somebody was watching me. But every time I turned around, everyone behind me was just going about their day. I admit it was busy, but I didn't recognise anyone. It was the strangest thing. Maybe I'm just not getting enough sleep or I don't know... The meeting at the lawyers went well, as I told you, but perhaps it's just the stress of buying the club. I don't know."

Alison nodded, still watching her. Victoria wasn't one to stress about business and the purchase of the club wasn't an enormous commitment, financially or otherwise. They'd put a manager in place and had their usual digital marketing team on the case to drive bookings. Victoria kept referring to it as a club, but it was an old building they were repurposing as a multifunctional venue space. It had at one time been an old candle factory, before a book binding firm took it over. The idea of so much creativity across the years fascinated Alison. But it didn't stress her, nor should it be stressing Victoria. Even if the enterprise flopped, it wouldn't be a big enough blow to alter their lifestyles.

As they pulled off the quiet road up the long driveway to reach the Aberdour Airbnb, Alison and Victoria twisted in their seats, watching the little blue car carry on towards the next village of Crossview. They both gave a simultaneous sigh of relief.

"This paranoia thing is infectious." She gave Victoria a wink as the car pulled into the front of the property. They were literally dropping off supplies for their client's decorators who were about to turn the place into a haunted house of kink for the next three days. Alison was fairly sure the couples who'd be arriving later that day wouldn't be bobbing for apples.

Victoria had sold them a bonus package which included, but was not limited to, three hundred condoms, four litres of lube, and a variety of toys, all of which came from their adult website, so it was an easy win for them. Alison swung open the rear door of the Defender, pulling out the first box and handing it to Abby. As she swung around ready to hand the second box to Victoria, she was met with a ringtone and Victoria's hand halting her.

"I need to take this, sorry."

Alison sighed and rolled her eyes as she watched Victoria accept the call. It wasn't until she came back for more boxes did she realise that something was wrong. Victoria's face was pale, her expression grave.

"I understand. When?"

Alison stopped in her tracks. She knew Victoria well enough to understand the edge in her tone. It was fear.

"Are you sure?" She said it almost as if there was a glimmer of hope that the person on the other end might be wrong in whatever information they were offering. "But how? I…I don't understand how."

Several seconds passed and Victoria's hand moved to her hairline, grabbing a handful of hair. Whatever this was,

Alison thought, watching Victoria's telltale stress response, it sure as hell wasn't good news.

"Okay, when? Just tell me when. Monday? But that was three days ago. She could be—"

Curiosity was piqued in Alison. *She could be? Who was* she?

"Okay, if you hear anything else, let me know." Victoria took the phone and stopped the call. Alison stared, certain her eyes reflected the panic she was seeing in Victoria's.

"Who was that?" she asked.

Victoria let out a long sigh again, pushing back the hair from her face to reveal the full weight of the stress she was obviously feeling. "It was Gareth."

"Why is Gareth calling you?"

Victoria turned to her, expression stony. "Mhairi's back."

Chapter 7
ALISON

Alison slumped into the chair opposite her therapist, offering a long sigh. There was a pause as she waited for Olivia's opening line—not that Alison thought the woman was predictable—but there was something reassuringly inevitable about the way she opened every session, asking "so what do you want to talk about today?". But that wasn't what Olivia said.

"At our last session, you talked about the bond that Victoria and Abby share and how you'd like to feel that connection with someone. Have you thought more about that?"

The question threw Alison, and she let it hang in the air as she tried to gather her thoughts. That hadn't been what she'd expected to talk about. Did she still want someone of her own? Would anyone want her in that way?

With Mhairi potentially emerging again from the depths, Alison could hardly consider herself to be a decent relationship prospect for anyone. Who in their right mind would take on that level of baggage? Certainly not Olivia. Her therapist was far too level-headed. She also knew far too much about Alison to see her for anything other than she was—damaged goods.

Pain tightened across her chest. Now wasn't the time to say any of that, not when she was being handed a much easier route to take. So she simply gave the truth, albeit a shallower version of the chasm of thoughts which belied it. "Yes, I still want someone of my own. It doesn't mean that I don't love Victoria and Abby. I do, but I want to know what it's like to have that deep connection with someone."

"You've never had that before?" Olivia seemed almost hopeful in the way she asked the question.

"No. I mean, I don't know what they're feeling, obviously, but I've not felt what I imagine they have." Alison paused, inhaling deeply and staring up towards the corner of the room. "A connection so deep that you lose all rationale; so consuming that normal rules can't touch you because when you're together, you're invincible."

Olivia took in a sharp breath, and Alison watched as she gripped her pen tighter. "And would you say you stayed within the rules when you were with Mhairi?"

"That was completely different. They weren't *our* rules, they were hers, and *we* weren't invincible. She just saw herself as invincible. I was just…collateral damage." Alison snorted in disgust. "We've been through all this. I'm not interested in recreating my past mistakes."

Olivia gave a nod, as though understanding she needed to move on. "And you don't get that feeling of invincibility with Victoria and Abby?"

Alison sighed, taking a long breath. "On Monday, I didn't get back until late. I'd been with clients all day and the house was quiet. I thought perhaps they had gone out for dinner, but then I heard them in bed." Pulling at the edge of her cuff, she was suddenly aware of an uncomfortable niggle in the pit of her stomach. Leaning over, she crossed her arms tightly over her chest. A few beats passed, and neither of them spoke. It was only then that Alison realised she was rocking her body, albeit she hoped the motion was imperceptible to Olivia. The niggle was vulnerability. "I could have gone in and joined them, but I didn't. I went to my room, and I listened."

"Did they know you were in the house?"

"No."

"And what did you hear?"

"Them making love."

Olivia leant forward, resting her arms on her notepad, giving Alison her complete attention.

"And how did that make you feel?"

"Aroused." Alison met Olivia's eyes. "I touched myself— but I wasn't thinking about them as I made myself come."

Olivia's eyes widened, and she swallowed. Alison knew she didn't need to say anymore. She was pretty sure Olivia was way too nervous to ask the obvious question, so she allowed the lightest of smiles to play on her lips, and then moved on.

"But afterwards, I heard them talking and I know I shouldn't have, but I crept into the hall so I could hear them. I heard my name, and I was just curious."

Olivia seemed to narrow her eyes, waiting for Alison to continue, so she did.

"Abby was saying she felt guilty because they hadn't included me, but it didn't bother me. Then Victoria said that she shouldn't expect me to be there all the time anyway, that maybe I wouldn't want them after a while."

Olivia gave a slow nod. "Was that hard to hear?"

"It surprised me." Alison shrugged. "I mean, I know I'm not sure what I want, but I didn't think Victoria…" Alison's voice drifted off.

"Do you think she might be right?" asked Olivia.

"I don't know. Maybe. I think it's too soon for me to know what I want, but I think Victoria knows that. I'm just hoping I'm not causing her stress because I don't know what I want. Christ…I just don't know." Frustration made the pitch of Alison's voice rise.

"Why do you think you'd be stressing Victoria?" Olivia asked. "She doesn't seem to be somebody who would stress easily. From what you've said, she's usually in control, even with you and Abby."

Her therapist smiled with the last words, but Alison couldn't reflect her smile back. She was thinking about Mhairi again. She really would have to tell Olivia.

"It's not me she's stressing about," Alison blurted. "Mhairi's back." Alison sat, watching her therapist's eyebrows shoot up.

"How? When? Are you safe?" Her therapist's questions came out in quick succession.

"I don't know," Alison shrugged.

"I thought you said she was in a Thai jail?"

"She was, but the local police here got a report from Interpol. According to Victoria's contact, she came in via ferry. They'd tracked her through Europe but have been one step behind. They have found three aliases so far, the last one being used to buy tickets from Ireland across to Troon. She's been here for three days now, and we've just found out."

As if on instinct, Olivia moved forward in her seat and took Alison's hand. "You need to stay safe."

Alison gave a tight smile. She had no idea what Mhairi would do or why she would willingly come back. The only thing she knew was that she'd want money, because that's what Mhairi always wanted: money and power.

Chapter 8
DR OLIVIA HOPKINS

Gosier, the five star French restaurant in the centre of Edinburgh, was busy with patrons, far busier than Olivia expected it to be on November the fifth. She had anticipated a quiet evening with a handful of her single colleagues. Those with families were out at a variety of firework displays across the city. They'd be eating hotdogs or burgers or maybe candy floss as brightly coloured explosions burst overhead. It's partly why they'd arranged the meal for that night. Together, they wouldn't feel the sting of being single and childless. But sitting at the table, she wasn't joining in the conversation as she'd normally do, because all she could think about was Alison. Was she okay? A shudder went through her body at the mere thought of Mhairi getting close to her. Hadn't she suffered enough?

The sommelier, a young chap by the name of Stefan, brought across their wine. Olivia knew him well. Oddly, he'd been in a similar situation to Alison. His wife had been the domme in their relationship too, although she had been nowhere as evil as Mhairi. But neither was it as healthy as the relationship Alison described with Victoria. Olivia had helped him during the six months he'd come for counselling sessions. She had the same arrangement with all her clients, current or past: Olivia would never acknowledge them in public unless they acknowledged her first. Stefan always did, making sure he topped up her wine a little more generously than anyone else at the table.

Olivia returned his smile and then toyed with the cassoulet in front of her. The overpriced rustic plate of chicken, beans and shallots didn't interest her. Only Alison was given that privilege.

"Olivia, are you okay?" asked Gemma, her closest colleague and confidant.

Olivia smiled weakly and nodded. "I'm fine, I'm fine. Just a little tired, perhaps. It's been a long week."

Her colleague narrowed her eyes and nodded. Olivia wasn't sure if Gemma believed her, but confidant or not, there were some things that she couldn't share, and Gemma was wise enough to know when not to pry.

It was only as Stefan turned to leave and she looked in his direction, did she see the two women sitting at the table in the far corner. Olivia nearly dropped her fork. There was Victoria. Victoria and…her heart nearly stopped. Was it Alison? Sitting taller in her seat, Olivia strained to see. But the woman opposite Victoria wasn't Alison. This woman was older and sturdier. Whoever she was, it wasn't Abby because Alison had already described Abby as younger, with mousy waves. She talked so eloquently about the young woman that even though Olivia had never seen her, she could picture her in her mind. That wasn't Abby.

Olivia continued to stare. Just then, Victoria glanced around and Olivia shrank back. She did not know why she was hiding. It wasn't as though Victoria could recognise her. The woman Alison called *Mistress* didn't know who she was. Even so, she had an urge to disappear, to melt into the high-backed seat, frightened that Victoria might lay her eyes on her. Lifting her wineglass to her mouth, she sipped gently, peering over the rim. She was once again back in covert mode. The two women laughed and joked with hands touching fleetingly. They obviously knew each other well, and they enjoyed each other's company.

Victoria threw her head back, allowing wisps of red hair to fall back towards her shoulders. Then she shrugged as if apologising, rising from the chair. Olivia watched. Victoria was heading to the bathroom and in a split second she put down her wine glass, took her napkin off her lap and followed. They were going to have an accidental meeting, she'd decided.

"Are you sure you're okay?" Gemma called after her.

"I'm fine," Olivia blurted, desperate not to be distracted from her mission. Bursting into the ladies' room, the first thing that hit Olivia was the strong floral scent. The air freshener had obviously gone into overdrive. There were three cubicles. One was occupied while the other two appeared empty, doors ajar. They were alone. Flustered and unsure what to do, she turned on the tap to wash her hands. So far, she'd only seen Victoria at a distance, but this was a chance to see the woman up close. The woman who controlled Alison's sexual pleasure, her mistress. Her heart jumped as the latch on the cubicle door pulled back, allowing the door to swing open. Olivia turned to see the emerging redhead. Victoria was stunning. Mesmerised, Olivia found herself unable to speak, or do anything except awkwardly stare.

Victoria glanced down at Olivia's hands. "Is it one version of Happy Birthday you're supposed to sing to yourself as you wash your hands these days, or have they taken it up to two?" Her words came with a warm smile, but Olivia, uncharacteristically nervous, simply giggled in return, making the moment far more awkward than it needed to be.

There was a sense of relief when Victoria finished drying her hands on the thick cotton hand towel and left. Olivia cringed, waves of mortification descending over her cheeks. But now, at least on her own again, she could breathe. No wonder this fire-haired goddess had the devotion of both Alison and Abby.

Several moments later Olivia was still trying to get her legs to stop shaking and by the time she'd regained enough composure to make it back to her table, Victoria and her companion were shrugging on their jackets, about to leave; obviously they weren't staying for dinner. Victoria's date kissed her goodbye, a light peck on each cheek before turning her attention to Stefan. The other woman and Stefan obviously knew each other.

Curiosity ate away at her until she bid her colleagues good night. If Stefan knew the woman, he could tell her who she was, but... Olivia ran the strap of her bag through her fingers, worrying the stiff leather against skin. To ask him the burning question would be crossing another boundary, and worse still, she'd be pulling an innocent party into her bizarre game. It would be wrong, she would be abusing their previous therapeutic relationship for her own gain.

No, she couldn't do that, could she? Perhaps if she gave him a choice? She wouldn't be insisting he told her who the woman was. Olivia wasn't his therapist any longer, she was his... Olivia paused, unwilling to classify the connection between her and Stefan because doing so might stop her from doing what she already knew was wrong. If the information Stefan could provide would help her better understand Alison then was it really so wrong? Olivia would just be a curious customer, and if he refused her the details then she'd accept it gracefully, leaving him with an apology.

Olivia had never before stepped out of the ethical confines to which she was bound. To do such a thing had been unthinkable but then she'd met Alison.

"Stefan," Olivia called as the sommelier cleared away the glasses from a table whose guests had just departed.

"Yes, Dr Hopkins?"

"Olivia, please. It's been so long since, well…" Olivia knew the moment she stripped herself of her title she had also obliterated the boundary between them. The boundary which was there to keep him (and her) safe but she couldn't stop herself.

"Stefan, I wouldn't normally do this, and I know we've always agreed that we wouldn't publicly acknowledge each other, but I need to ask you a question. You don't have to answer it, obviously, and it's not of any great importance,"—Olivia drew in a long breath knowing she was about to throw herself off a cliff—"but there were two women here earlier, sitting at that table over there. You seemed to know one of them and I just...I know this is an odd question, but who was she?" Olivia held her breath. *Was it really so wrong to ask?* She knew the answer, but her compulsion to find a way of getting closer to Alison was overriding her otherwise characteristic rationale.

Stefan smiled. "Her name is Jenny Myles. She runs a…a club of sorts for people who…well—you know what I like." Stefan stopped, offering a shy smile.

Olivia knew exactly what he liked. Kink, of a very serious variety. She nodded.

"Jenny puts people like me and others in touch with each other. Like a kinky dating agency." Stefan chuckled.

"Oh." Olivia couldn't stop herself. "Could you put me in touch with her?" she asked.

Stefan's eyes went wide. "You? Why would…? Oh, okay. Yes, I-I can do that."

"Good," Olivia said. "Can you give me her details now?"

Stefan nearly burst out laughing. "You're eager. Yes, just give me a moment." He disappeared over to the side, taking his phone from the drawer next to the ordering centre. Olivia said good night to the stragglers from her table, eager to usher them out the door before Stefan came back. When he appeared again, it was to hand her a small white card, with a name and number in blue ink. The first line of block capitals read, 'Jenny Myles' and underneath it was a mobile number.

Chapter 9
VICTORIA

"Bryce, I'm putting you on speakerphone," Victoria said, waving her hands to usher Abby and Alison closer. "Bryce, repeat what you told me so Abby and Alison can hear."

Abby put down her laptop and wandered over to the kitchen island where Victoria had placed the phone. Alison put her glass down and leant forward on her elbows, ready to listen intently.

"Are they there?" Bryce's voice rose from the granite island top.

"Yes. Go on, tell them."

"You're going to be the main feature in the Christmas edition. We're going to be doing a full centre spread. I spoke to our creative director and we like what you've done so much that we're ditching the piece on eproctophilia. Plus, to give you centre stage. I'm not sure the sound effect would have worked anyway, but that's by the by. And Abby?"

"Y-yeah," Abby said nervously.

"Your images are incredible, according to our creative director, Phillipe. I'm just as impressed. But Phillipe was speechless, and trust me when I say that's a first."

Abby blushed. Victoria was beaming at her. Alison even jumped up and down in glee, silently clapping her hands.

"And the flick book images are inspiring. That's the exact word Phillipe used. *Inspiring*. He wondered if you'd be interested in doing some other work for us?"

Abby immediately looked at Victoria. Victoria raised her eyebrows and hands in a shrug that said, *it's your call,* because that's exactly what she was thinking. If Abby wanted to do this, she would not stand in her way. In fact, if there was anything she could do to support Abby in her choices, she'd be the first one to help.

"Umm, let's talk. It depends what you have in mind," Abby said. "But I'm happy to talk about anything that might come up."

They finished the call and Bryce promised Phillipe would be in touch. Victoria pulled Abby into an enormous hug.

"I knew you were the person for this job," she giggled. "I'm thrilled for you."

Alison was laughing too. "Victoria, you just didn't want to get into that outfit in front of strangers."

Victoria blushed. There was some truth in what Alison said. She brushed it aside to focus on Bryce's words that piqued her interest.

"What was Bryce talking about when he mentioned the *flick book?*"

"Oh, it's nothing, just a cute idea I had." Abby shrugged off any further conversation and changed the subject. "I need to head into town. The stockist has a new lens for me. I won't be long. Maybe about an hour?" Lifting her laptop, she glanced around, looking for her satchel.

Victoria grimaced. "I'm not sure I like you going into town on your own, not just now. We still don't have a fix on Mhairi yet and—I don't want her coming near you. Alison, could you…?"

Alison shrugged. "Uh-huh. I'm not doing anything. I'll come along if you want some company. I can't drive, though." She held up the half full glass of wine. "But I can fend off overzealous traffic wardens."

"Great," Abby said. "I've just got to grab one or two things from the studio and I'll meet you at the car?"

"Sure, just give me two minutes." Alison swept out of the room happily.

"Thank you for taking her along. I feel better knowing that neither of you are on your own." Victoria placed her hands on Abby's shoulders and then kissed her forehead. "I'm so proud of you."

"I know." Flashing a cheeky grin, Abby placed a fleeting kiss against her lips. "Catch you later. Enjoy your paperwork."

Left alone in the room, Victoria pulled up a stool and sat down at the island, her MacBook on hand, ready to work her way through the volume of emails sitting in her inbox. She sighed, clicking on Bryce's confirmation of their earlier conversation. He just needed their go-ahead in writing for the feature but before she could open the DocuSign link, her phone lit up.

Jenny's name popped up on the screen. Lifting the phone to her ear, she immediately heard Jenny's soft lilt.

"Are you busy?"

Victoria glanced at her inbox, proudly displaying fifty unread messages, and smiled. "No. I'm not busy."

"Good, I've got a favour to ask. Do you remember Stefan? You know the sommelier from Gosier? The one who's into claustrophilia and had his way with the weightlifting Russian in the boot of that Fiat 500?"

Victoria gave an *Uh-huh*, wondering where exactly Jenny was going with this conversation.

"Well, he passed my number onto this journalist friend of

his who wants to do a piece on the Mistresses of Edinburgh, and I immediately thought of you."

Victoria frowned. "Why not you, Jenny?" she asked with curiosity.

"Mm. I can't. Love to, but I can't. She wants to talk to somebody this week, and I'm about to fly out to Magaluf on a spanking weekend. Plus, she has a particular interest in all things polyamorous."

There was a beat of silence as Victoria considered this odd request. The journalist had a very well-defined checklist, but without giving her any longer to think about it, Jenny spewed more information.

"It's all about the rise of the femdoms. I think it's going to be an empowering piece she's after, but she's very curious. I think you might have fun with her."

Victoria smiled, unsure of quite what Jenny meant by having fun with her, but she agreed to give the woman a call. Anything that took her mind off Mhairi would be a welcome distraction. Unless—could this be related to Mhairi in some way?

Chapter 10
ALISON

Alison pushed open the door to Abby's studio, which was ajar, and leant against the doorframe. She watched the young woman bent over the old oak bench, staring down intently at some black and white images. There was something fascinating about watching Abby when she was so engrossed in her work. She hadn't seen Alison; she hadn't even been aware she was there, and absently she tucked a few strands of her mousy brown hair that had fallen from her high ponytail behind her ear. Alison could stand and watch Abby work like this all day. She was beautiful, far more beautiful than the young woman realised, but right now she had to find Victoria.

"Have you seen Victoria?"

Abby jumped. "What?"

Alison smiled. "Sorry, didn't mean to give you a fright, I just wondered if you'd seen Victoria. I went across to the house but she wasn't there."

"Oh," said Abby. "She had an appointment with the lawyers. They wanted to see her about the club, so she left just after breakfast. She said we weren't to expect her back before dinner."

Alison nodded absently. "What's that smell?"

Abby wrinkled her nose. "It's the fixer for the prints."

The week previous, Abby had the finishing touches put on a darkroom she had installed in the corner of her studio. While Victoria wanted her to prioritise some form of heating, Abby had rebelled, insisting a darkroom was far more important.

"Thank god for that," said Alison. "I thought you'd taken in some incontinent geriatrics. It smells like one of those badly run care homes you hear about on the news."

Abby chuckled. "Well, that's rich coming from somebody who virtually dabs paint stripper behind their ears."

"Very true. We have far too much in common. That we enjoy working in the smell of ammonia is just one of them." Alison enjoyed the carefree banter she shared with Abby. It was a far cry from her life with Mhairi, where every word she'd said had been analysed, criticised, and scorned. Walking on eggshells had become the norm until the shallow breathing that accompanied it had almost suffocated her.

"Can I help?" Abby asked, turning away again to look back at the images in front of her.

Alison wasn't sure if she actually meant it, or if she was just being polite, but she needed somebody to assist her. "I just finished the piece. You know, the framework I was working on? Normally I get Victoria to test the new pieces out with me, but if she's not here… You don't have five, ten, twenty minutes, do you?"

Alison knew she was pushing her luck because Abby had been moaning last night about deadlines, but she reckoned, no cheek, no chance. This was a big commission and, as a natural perfectionist, she wanted it thoroughly tested.

Abby eyed her suspiciously. "Exactly what do you want me to do?"

"Well…strip down to your underwear, let me tie you up and then pull you into various sexual positions. Just the usual afternoon stuff."

"Oh, thank god for that," said Abby. "I thought you were going to ask me to do something weird. Yeah, I can give you ten minutes."

————

Alison was making some final adjustments to the harness when Abby walked in, announcing her arrival with a "Wow!"

"I forgot you haven't been in since I started putting this together. Impressive, isn't it?"

Abby nodded, her expression somewhere between shock and trepidation. This was the first time she'd been in Alison's studio in over two weeks, although she'd asked Alison several times what all the banging, thumping and general swearing was about. Their studios shared one adjoining wall and usually Abby would have just wandered around to find out for herself, but Alison had kept the door closed to give her the peace to complete this project.

"I put the heaters on so it's warm, not like your place. When I said I needed you to strip down, I wasn't joking. I need to know if the harness tightens correctly and won't cause any chafing."

Abby gave her a wry smile and duly pulled her sweater over her head. To Alison's surprise, the young woman wasn't wearing a bra. Inhaling deeply, she realised that all of her concentration would have to be placed in stopping herself from getting distracted. Between fantasising about Olivia, and her ongoing appreciation of Abby, she was behaving like a hormonal teenager.

"Thanks for warming the place up." Abby stood in a pair of tiny red cotton pants. Designed to be more functional than alluring, Alison still found the sight arousing—very understated and quite demure. Very Abby. "They look like monkey bars." Abby ran her hands over one set of the thick wood pillars which ran up to the framework above. "So, how does this work?"

"These wires attach to a harness, which you'll wear. There's a wire for each of your limbs, and another for head support. I attach the wires to these tracks embedded in the wood." She pointed to silver runners cased within the wood, pulling the wire to show how it moved. "Then I use this,"—Alison held up the small remote, not dissimilar to a Firestick remote—"to tighten the wire, which lifts your arms or legs."

Abby walked forward, laying an arm over Alison's shoulder, gazing at the tiny black gadget as the wire moved within the metal track. The heat between their bodies seemed to spark, or at least it did for Alison, who straightened up, allowing Abby's arm to slide away. Victoria had made the rules of their relationship very clear. While Victoria could take either of her subs where and whenever she wanted (with their consent), the only time that Abby and Alison could be together intimately was in Victoria's presence, and under her instruction.

It was a rule that she found hard to focus on as she watched Abby slide her hands down her sides and inside the elastic of her cotton pants. Alison looked away.

"I'm operating you a bit like a puppet, so I can make you parallel to the floor, upright or upside down, and everything in between. Basically, you relinquish all control. Only I can move your body—into whatever position I want to take you." Alison's breath hitched.

Abby gave a slow grin, obviously enjoying the effect she was having on her. *Was Abby fucking with her? Christ, if only.*

Clearing her throat, Alison grabbed the tangle of light-weight restraints. "Can you come over here?" The harness had straps that supported one side of each limb with a soft bamboo mesh. Thinner straps wound around the limb, holding them in place and allowing the D-Hooks to be aligned to the awaiting wires. "Okay, I need you to stand in a star shape, almost as if you were about to go onto a big diagonal St Andrew's Cross." Carefully she wrapped each strap into place over Abby's firm skin, taking a little longer than was absolutely necessary.

"They're softer than I thought they'd be. The straps I mean."

Alison knelt in front of Abby, allowing her to place her hands on Alison's shoulders. Without having to ask, Abby widened her stance, allowing Alison access to her inner thighs, making it easier to secure the binding. "Your hands are warm."

Alison swallowed and tried desperately to concentrate. The scent of arousal filled her senses. At least she wasn't the only one who was getting turned on, she mused, fighting the urge to sink her face into Abby's obvious excitement.

"Okay, so arms and legs are secure. I just need to put in the support for your neck. It secures—" Alison held the wide strip of mesh, one end in each hand and stared at Abby's nipples. Flushed rose pink and erect, they seemed to vibrate with readiness. Breathing heavily, she ran her tongue over her bottom lip. Slowly, very slowly, she raised her eyes to meet Abby's. They were dark, pupils blown wide, probably a reflection of her own.

"I need to place this around—just under your…" She lifted her hands towards Abby's rib cage. Wrapping her arms around Abby's torso, she secured the last support in place, her mouth accidentally brushing against those erect nipples she'd drooled over seconds earlier. *I can't,* she told herself.

54

"You shouldn't be wearing clothes," Abby blurted. "Just a strap-on."

"I-I—" Alison knew the word she was looking for. It was, *No.* But there wasn't a chance in hell the word 'no' was about to come slipping from between her lips. In three seconds flat her clothes were off and she was swearing as she tried to unravel the thin PVC straps so she could slide her legs into place.

"It's the only way we can really test it out, right?" she said a moment later, stepping towards Abby and running her hand over the length of the shaft.

Abby nodded, eyes fixed on Alison as, with one flick of the remote, she lifted off the floor.

Stepping between Abby's legs, which were stretched so wide apart the red cotton offered little to no coverage, a rush of exhilaration swept through Alison's body, filling her chest and making her feel lightheaded. It was unlike anything she'd felt before. This wasn't just sexual arousal. This was the euphoria of power.

Running her fingers over the damp red gusset of Abby's pants, she felt the pulse of her swollen clit and smiled as the younger woman moaned in pleasure.

"So if I lower the angle," she said, bringing Abby's centre down so it pressed against the tip of the dildo, "then I could just slide right in." The silicon nudged aside the thin layer of cotton and Abby moaned again, but instead of pushing inside, Alison simply rubbed the toy over the length of Abby's desire.

"Inside. Please." Abby panted with a desperation unlike Alison had heard before. A jolt of electricity coursed through her body. *Hell, was this what Victoria felt when they made love?* There was no doubt she wanted to give Abby what she was practically begging for, being the one in control of that gratification was intoxicating. But not so intoxicating that it meant defying Victoria.

"I won't." Her voice was quiet, but still she slid the slick silicon against Abby's entrance.

"Please," Abby whimpered.

Alison didn't know what she wanted more, to fuck Abby or revel in the potency of withholding pleasure.

What would Victoria do? Victoria!

Alison stepped back, horrified that they had come so close to breaking the rules.

"Abby, we can't. I'm sorry. We can't do this without Victoria's instruction." She looked down at the strap-on glistening with Abby's excitement. "This is my fault. I shouldn't have put you in that position."

"Alison?"

"No, please don't say anything. I was being selfish. I just—I really wanted to take you, and I don't know—"

"Alison!"

"Yeah?" Alison glanced up, her face heavy with guilt.

"Are you going to let me down? Literally."

Chapter 11
VICTORIA

The buzzer on the entrance door sounded angry, impatient, as though it was giving an order to the occupant to hurry. There had been no name assigned to the flat, just the number 2B. In the New Town Georgian flats of Edinburgh, that meant it was the second of the two flats on the first floor. 1A and 1B would have taken up the ground floor. The communal stair was clean, with original tiles decorating the outside edges of the door frames. There was the slightest hint of bleach in the air, and the second door had a small display of pumpkins neatly piled on a bed of straw. A chalkboard sign with big white lettering stuck in the middle read, 'Trick or Treat'.

Victoria glanced up as the creak of an opening door echoed through the hall from above. There had been a point when she considered cancelling the request to see the journalist, or at the very least contacting Gareth to do a background check, but she couldn't get a police background check done on every new person she came across, even if the timing was rather coincidental. Instead, she had just got her

57

new PA, Laura, to check out the person she'd agreed to meet. The info she'd come back with was innocuous enough to know there was no need to change her plans. In fact, armed with more details, Victoria was looking forward to this encounter.

A woman in a dark dress emblazoned with large, bright flowers stood in the open doorway. She hadn't been what Victoria had expected. The request to meet and the subject had been bold, but the fair-haired woman seemed almost timid, and certainly a little unsure of herself.

"You must be Kerry Patterson?" The rise in Victoria's voice conveyed her surprise. Kerry Patterson was the name Jenny had given her, the same name the woman confirmed on the phone...and the name that Laura had researched, but...

"Yes. Victoria Fraser, I presume." The woman smiled. "Please come in."

Intrigue trumped caution as Victoria followed the fair-haired woman. The flat was simply furnished and decorated in neutral tones, and the large sitting room was light and airy thanks to the large windows that looked out onto the street below. Victoria noted the slightest hint of jasmine, which seemed to follow the woman as she led them to two large sofas dominating the room.

"Can I get you something to drink?" she asked.

Victoria shook her head. "No, I'm fine, thanks. Shall we sit?"

The woman nodded, sitting at one end and allowing Victoria to sit at the opposite. Victoria hooked one leg under the other, turning her body to face the woman. She was attractive, if not a little awkward, with a pale complexion and beautiful strawberry blonde waves that framed her face.

"So you want to talk to me about the rise of the...what

was it you said? The femdom?" Victoria allowed a smile to play on her lips as she watched the woman blush. "Not to be mistaken with the Femidom."

The woman let out a small giggle, blushing more. *She's certainly cute,* Victoria thought, never once releasing the woman from her gaze. After a beat of silence, the woman spoke.

"No. You're quite funny." The woman caught Victoria's gaze and pulled herself a little straighter, as though she'd remembered why they were there. "I want to understand what it takes to be a domme, to understand the lifestyle. I think that's the right expression, isn't it?"

Victoria nodded.

"Then yes, I want to understand the lifestyle and what it means to be you."

"Me?" Victoria chuckled.

"Jenny assures me you are the epitome of the femdom."

Victoria smiled. "Jenny is too generous, by far. But I'm curious, why do you want to write about this and why now? My research indicated that you're an investigative journalist. Wasn't your last big article about the rise of ethnic gangs in Glasgow? From what I read, you yourself were the subject of death threats. The rise of the femdom seems lightweight in comparison—unless, of course, you have some sort of angle on the subject? Perhaps one that's less than favourable?"

Victoria was sure she saw the slightest flicker of panic in the woman's eyes before she replaced it with a shy smile. This was proving to be one of the most interesting meetings Victoria had experienced in a long time.

"Ms. Fraser, when you've been looking over your shoulder for as many months as I have, sometimes a 'quirky' article is a welcome break from the usual grittiness I face. Surely you can't blame me for wanting a little light relief?

Plus, I think readers will be as intrigued as I am about your lifestyle. From what Jenny tells me, you are in a polyamorous relationship."

"Mm." Victoria liked the quick-witted way the woman redirected the conversation with ease, but she wasn't ready to open up yet until she had uncovered the real agenda in play.

"And where would this piece be published? Who are you proposing to sell it to?" she asked.

"As you've already found out, I'm freelance, so I have several options…" The woman faltered as though she was working out what to say next, but Victoria wasn't prolonging this any longer.

"Shall we cut to the chase?" she said. "Kerry, are you interested in writing an article or do you have desires of your own you wish to explore under the guise of journalism?"

The woman blushed. It started at her neck and worked up, covering her cheeks until she shone like a scarlet beacon.

"You wouldn't be the first to have come up with a ruse in order to talk to me, but I appreciate honesty. Now would be the time for *your* honesty."

"No, I am…I'm writing a piece. I am writing something." The woman flailed. "I just…it's something I've always been curious about, and having the opportunity to talk to you about it perhaps, then yes, it's a bit of both."

Victoria nodded, contemplating her next move. "Is that your whole truth, Kerry?" she asked.

The woman nodded, her cheeks still burning bright. The afternoon was turning out to be far more entertaining than Victoria thought possible, but it was nothing compared to how much fun she was about to have.

"Okay, I'll tell you what I'll do. I'll allow you an insight into our lifestyle, but only on certain conditions."

The woman's expression was serious, her eyes wide. She nodded.

"These are non-negotiable. So you either agree or walk away. Understood?"

Again, the woman nodded.

"Do you see yourself as dominant or submissive?" Victoria asked in the same tone as someone would if they were enquiring if you took sugar in your coffee. Matter of fact.

"Dominant. Definitely dominant. I need to—"

"Need to?" Victoria asked.

"I want to be you," the woman blurted.

Victoria eyed her curiously. This woman was much farther down the rabbit hole of desire than she'd realised. This was far too much fun to be morally right.

"Okay, but you have to understand in order to be a good domme, a good mistress, you need to understand how to be a good sub. So if you really want to learn, then I'll take you under my wing and I'll teach you how to be a sub. From there, you can decide if you have what it takes to be a mistress."

Victoria's face was poker straight as she looked at the woman, who now seemed decidedly nervous. "Do we have a deal?" Victoria asked, her tone measured.

"Yes, we have a deal."

"Good," said Victoria. Then, picking up her bag and standing, she said, "I have your number. I'll be in touch with instructions on what will happen next. Is this your preferred address for packages? I may have the occasional item I need to send to you."

"W-what will you send?" The tremor in the woman's voice made Victoria smile.

"Well, that's a surprise and if I tell you, it won't be a surprise. Now, is this the address?"

Victoria watched her nod.

"Good, then expect to hear from me. I'll see myself out." And with that, Victoria swept out and down the stairs, smiling to herself. This was going to come as a very welcome distraction.

Chapter 12
VICTORIA

Victoria hit the button to open the newly-fitted electric gates that sealed the entrance to their property. A small red flicker caught her eye. "Good," she said, her words echoing around the otherwise empty 4x4, "the cameras are up and running."

With Mhairi about, she was taking no chances. The enhanced security system meant they benefitted from the same level of protection as Buckingham Palace...or at least that's what the security consultant claimed. He'd at least had the integrity to blush when Victoria had pointed out that intruders had breached the monarch's home on several occasions.

"Perhaps you need to rethink your sales pitch," she suggested without a hint of irony, and then placed the expedited order. Tonight, she was thankful she'd taken steps to keep them safe.

Parking up, she looked at the house, which lay in darkness, and then over towards Abby's studio, where lights blazed. She turned off the engine and made her way across the wide gravelled path to the illuminated windows. It had been a productive and highly amusing day, but one she now had to explain to Abby. Victoria could only hope she'd understand.

"Honey, I'm home," she shouted, pushing open the door to Abby's studio and squinting against the super bright lights. Whenever she walked into Abby's space, it was always from one extreme to another. Either it was brighter than the surface of the sun, or so dimly lit with the reddish glow from the darkroom, you'd be forgiven for thinking you'd strayed to a less-than-salubrious alley in De Wallen.

"I'm over here." Abby's voice came from the other side of the room. She emerged from a large storage cupboard, squinting in the bright light of the room. "I was just getting everything together for tomorrow. Matt and I are doing a day of headshots at The Wealth Partnership."

"That sounds like fun." Victoria's reply was heavy with sarcasm. "Will it bring in enough to finally pay for heating?" Victoria shivered.

"I don't notice the cold when I'm working." Abby shrugged, and Victoria had to stifle a laugh. Her lover wore more layers than a Schichttorte. Even Alison, who was the hardiest of them all, had seen sense and linked her studio up to the Biomass system. But Abby wanted to pay for it herself, and she always found something more pressing to spend her earnings on.

"Where's Alison?" Victoria enquired. She rather hoped that she'd find Abby alone, not that she had anything sexual in mind. It was far too cold for that, but sometimes it was easier to chat when it was just the two of them.

"Uh, she's at a client's. Final prep for their installation, I think she said." Abby blushed. "Victoria, there's something I need to talk to you about. I—"

"Okay, but let me go first." Victoria took a breath and pulled out a stool from under Abby's workbench. "Come and join me for a minute."

Abby hesitated, then pulled out the second stool. "This sounds serious."

Victoria laid a hand on her shoulder. "Don't look so worried. It's something and nothing, really. I just had an *interesting* day."

"Interesting?" Abby screwed her face up and cocked her head. "In what way?"

"I met somebody and…" Victoria paused. "Jenny asked me to talk to her. She's a journalist writing a piece about female dominatrixes. Something about the power and rise of Scottish 'femdoms'. Anyway, I met her on the pretence of an interview, but it didn't turn out that way."

Abby raised an eyebrow.

"Yeah. I've agreed to teach her how to be a domme, but of course that starts with being a good sub."

Abby's eyes widened. "What?"

"It's not hands-on training, don't worry."

"Wait. Victoria, what are you saying?"

"Well, if she wants to write this piece and get it accurate, then the best way of doing that is to experience it."

Abby crossed her arms over her chest and scowled. "You decided to introduce somebody new and I'm just supposed to suck it up?"

Victoria laughed, then caught Abby's glare. "Sorry, that was childish. The *suck it up* was oddly amusing."

"This isn't funny, Victoria." Abby's tone echoed her words, and Victoria knew immediately she had miscalculated her approach.

Victoria went to take Abby's hand, but the younger woman pulled it away. Holding up palms in mock surrender, she tried to explain. "I'm not introducing anybody new."

"So you're excluding me? You meet up somewhere for a quick shag, but don't worry, Abby, it's just part of the government apprenticeship scheme." Abby stood and

Victoria caught her wrist, refusing to allow her to storm away.

Victoria knew what she was doing, and naively she'd expected Abby to be on the same wavelength, but that obviously wasn't the case.

"Abby, darling, I will not lay a finger on her. I would never touch anyone without your consent. Hell, I've not even been with Alison without you being there, so I'm hardly—"

"Then how do you...train her?"

"There are lots of different ways to teach someone to be a sub. As long as she thinks that I'm dominant, then she will submit."

"So you won't touch her and she won't touch you?"

"No, but she will do what I tell her to."

"So you'll virtually seduce her? Fuck her by Zoom." Abby's brows knitted together. "I'm not sure I like that any better."

"No, I won't *fuck her by Zoom*, although that is quite an interesting concept in its own right. I was just thinking about a few texts. There is nothing sexual in this...not for me, at least. All I'm doing is teaching her how to surrender. You just need to trust me on this."

Abby looked more like a warrior about to go into action than a woman assured. There was something incredibly hot about this green-eyed monster which was emerging. It was a side of Abby that Victoria hadn't seen before.

"It's a big world out there, Abby, and there's more than one way of getting somebody to understand what it means to submit. But do you trust me? Because that's all that matters and if you don't, then I will tell her we're not doing this."

"Mm." Abby thought for a moment. "I want to see how you do it."

Victoria laughed. "You want me to show you how I'll get her to submit?"

"Uh-huh. I want to see it all. The texts, the messages, however you do it. I want to see it all."

Victoria nodded. "With her consent, I don't see why that should be a problem."

Abby snorted. "With her consent? You sure as shit didn't ask me for my consent before you agreed to this."

Victoria winced. Abby was right.

"I'm asking now. If you don't want me to do this, I won't. And Abby—I'm sorry. You're right. I should never have agreed to anything without discussing it with you first. But I'd have never done anything behind your back." Victoria shook her head. "I'd never jeopardise what we have, never." Victoria took Abby's hands in her own and squeezed them. "You're my entire world."

Pulling her closer, Victoria saw a single tear run down Abby's cheek. With her thumb, she whisked it away. "God, I'm sorry. I didn't want to hurt you. Let me call this off. I won't have you getting upset."

Victoria reached into her pocket and pulled out her phone.

"Wait." Abby sniffed. "Don't."

Victoria watched Abby slump against the chair, as though the jealousy and rage which had filled her body moments earlier had drained away, leaving her deflated.

"I need to tell you something, and you're not going to like it."

Chapter 13
VICTORIA

Victoria sat stunned, trying desperately to take in what Abby was telling her. If she had seen it coming, perhaps it wouldn't have come as such a punch in the gut. But had she? Had she seen it coming?

In the bedroom, Alison was becoming more assertive, almost a little brattish, but Victoria had thought the behaviour was attention-seeking. Perhaps to incite a punishment, but what Abby was describing was something altogether different.

"Tell me again what happened," Victoria demanded in a terse tone.

"Which bit?" Tears were streaming down Abby's face, and snot glistened against her top lip, but to Victoria she was still the most beautiful woman she had ever known.

"From the point she hoisted you up in the air like a bloody puppet."

"Victoria, Mistress, it's not her fault. She's the one that stopped—"

Victoria cut her off, her response measured but firm. "I don't think *Mistress* is appropriate right now, do you? You certainly weren't thinking about your *mistress* when you were begging Alison to fuck you. Were you?" The lack of emotion in her voice sounded chilling, even to her. The younger woman dropped to her knees in front of her.

"I'd do anything to take it back. I don't want her, I only want you. I'm so sorry." Abby's tears felt warm against her trousers, and as disappointed as she was, Victoria couldn't stop herself from soothing her lover. Stroking Abby's brown waves, Victoria swallowed back tears of her own. Everything had been so perfect, so right. Surrounded by the love of the two most important women in her life, Victoria had at times had to pinch herself to make sure it was all real. But now this.

"The rules keep us safe, Abby. All of us. They're not there for my amusement, or so I can exert arbitrary control over the two of you. This relationship works because we under- stand and protect the dynamics. It's a careful balance between need and want, power and control, and I don't mean my control as a mistress, but the control of desires we have for each other that's born out of respect."

Abby sobbed. Victoria heaved a heavy sigh. Ignoring this and sweeping it under the carpet as though it had never really happened wasn't an option. It had to be tackled head-on.

"Look at me." Victoria's voice remained calm. "I have always been honest with you—"

"So have I, that's why I told you," Abby pleaded, but was stopped as Victoria's finger touched her lips.

"Shh, now. Let me finish."

Abby gave a contrite nod.

"I need to know if you get everything you need from me, or whether Alison offers you something I can't." Victoria swallowed, unsure that she was ready to hear Abby's answer.

"You give me more than I need, and everything I could

ever want. It was just a moment of stupidity. Alison was in control, she was…she was like you… Victoria, I'm so sorry." Abby pushed her face into Victoria's knees again, shame radiating through sobs.

Victoria sat for several minutes, contemplating the subtle shifts in power which were gripping their relationship. What was she to do?

"Do you still want Alison?" Victoria's question seemed to confuse Abby, and she raised her head with a fearful gaze, as if searching for the right answer. "There's no right or wrong answer. All I want to hear is the truth," Victoria assured her.

"I-I love her, but not in the way I love you. Without you, I can't live. I only want you." Abby choked out the last words through hard sobs which racked her body. "Please don't send me away." The noise which followed was born out of a pain so deep it melted Victoria's heart. There was no way she could sit here and watch the woman she loved rip herself apart with anguish and guilt. The truth was, they hadn't broken the rules, not technically, and if she believed Abby, she had Alison to thank for that. But equally, as a dominatrix, she knew how easy it was to manipulate a scenario through emotion to gain the required outcome; it was why she analysed her own motivations so frequently.

A thought niggled at the back of her mind, one she didn't want to entertain. The abused may become the abuser. It was, in Victoria's opinion, a myth, peddled out in cases where victims hadn't been offered the correct support in order to heal; society's way of letting themselves off the hook for repeated failures of care. But Alison had controlled her desire, so that wasn't what was happening, Victoria assured herself.

"I'll do anything you want to make this right. Just tell me what to do," Abby begged.

"I'm not sending you away. You can get that out of your

head for a start." Victoria lifted Abby's chin, tilting her face up and locking eyes. At that moment, she knew exactly what she had to do. "If you want me to continue to be your mistress, then you need to behave like an obedient sub. Your desires are mine and mine alone. Do you understand?"

Abby nodded, sobs subsiding as her breathing became shallow. Victoria had Abby's entire attention, and she was about to reset the rules.

"I can't let this go unpunished, nor do I intend to. I demand complete devotion and if you can't offer me that, then say so now." Victoria watched as Abby's eyes darkened with arousal.

"You've my complete devotion, Mistress. I'll take any punishment you feel appropriate." Abby bowed her head, and as Victoria stroked her hair, she was sure she heard her purr.

Chapter 14

DR OLIVIA HOPKINS

Olivia hit return on the keyboard and pushed back from her desk. The notes for today's sessions were finished. It had been a long, hard day. Some days were easier than others, but today she chalked it up as 'tough'. Her phone buzzed, and without thinking, she picked it up. It was Sharon, her receptionist.

"Dr Hopkins, your husband's here."

Olivia sighed and rolled her eyes. "Sharon, he's not my husband."

"Mm," came the reply.

"He. Is. Not. My. Husband," she said again, punctuating every word with a full stop.

Sharon had been with the practice for over ten years, but she was a staunch Catholic and didn't believe in divorce. In Sharon's eyes, at least, and in the eyes of the *lord god almighty*, she told Olivia she'd be married until the day she died. It was taking a long time to get reality through to Sharon. They'd had similar issues a few years back when the older woman confronted a patient who had tried to die by their own hand. Her lack of compassion had nearly prompted the issuing of her P45, and her entry back into the job market. It always amazed Olivia how allegiance to a pay packet could alter people's fundamental beliefs.

"Very well. Dr Hopkins, Mr Lawson is here to see you."

"Thank you, Sharon." Olivia put down the phone just as the door opened and in walked a tall, attractive man. He had a shock of blonde hair, deep olive skin, and rich brown eyes. No matter how long or short it had been since she saw him last, Lucas always took her breath away. He was beyond aesthetically pleasing. Sadly, his personality wasn't as sparkling as his looks, and she'd found that out to her detriment after four years of marriage. To this day, she still couldn't get over how she'd managed four years with him. But she had.

"I'm not staying long," he announced. "This came for your sister at the flat. I thought you'd redirected all your mail."

She sighed again. "I had, Lucas, but there's one or two things of a more sensitive nature that Kerry needed to receive and she wanted them sent discreetly, so I suggested she use the flat address. I hope you don't mind?" Olivia didn't really care if he minded or not, as technically, the flat was still half hers.

"Discreetly?" he asked.

"It's work stuff. You don't need to worry."

"Mm." He paused for a moment and Olivia hoped he wouldn't press the matter. "Anyway, it had this big 'urgent' label on it, so I thought I'd better bring it round. Are there more things to come?"

Olivia looked blankly at him for a moment.

"You said one or two things. That means there might be more packages. Should I expect further deliveries?"

"I don't know. Is it a problem?"

"Umm, well no. No, I suppose it's not."

Lucas's flat was on the next street to Olivia's practice. It had been great when the two of them had been together because she could literally walk from home to work in a matter of minutes. But it had been two years since they split up, and now her commute was a good thirty minutes each way. But she had left Lucas, so she'd ended up in a small flat out at Portobello, while he existed comfortably in their New Town flat.

When she first moved she'd tried to console herself with the notion she had a view of the beach, but the reality was she had to stand on a small stool with her head out of the skylight to actually see any sand.

"Do you want to grab a drink?" she said to Lucas. They did still, occasionally, socialise together, mainly when he wanted to get a woman's take on his latest relationship disaster. The problem was Lucas had the charisma of a plant pot, and once women got past the "can you imagine how beautiful our children would be", there was little left to hold their interest. Given Lucas's sex drive made your average panda look horny, they moved past the whole question of breeding quickly. For Olivia, Lucas's lack of physical demands made their relationship last four whole years.

"Lucas, do you want to go for a drink?" she asked again, standing and slipping her mobile into her handbag.

"A drink? With you? No, no."

Olivia didn't take offence. For Lucas, who was usually blunt, his current exchange was verging on charming. "Okay." She sat back down, shaking her head. "Maybe another time."

"Mm," he said. "I'm going now."

"Thanks for dropping this in." Olivia picked up the small box, feeling the weight shift to the lowest point.

He nodded and, without saying another word, made for the door. He'd no doubt be anxious about trying to bypass Sharon and her twenty questions on the way out.

Gripping the box, she gave it a light shake. It seemed innocuous enough. A rectangle about six inches long, four inches wide, and about three inches deep, she reckoned. A white label with Lucas's address and Kerry Patterson's name had been placed in the centre. Turning it over in her hands, she looked for the most obvious seal and pulled apart the taped edges.

She hadn't looked at her phone since lunchtime. Perhaps now would be a good time to check for messages before she found out the parcel's contents. Swapping the box for her phone, she typed in her passcode and sure enough, there was a text from Victoria.

> I hope you like the present. You need to charge it first. I'll be expecting you to have them in place by tomorrow morning. Make sure everything is fitted correctly. I'll be in touch.

Curiosity getting the better of her, she put the phone down and lifted the box back up again, this time ripping it apart. *What the hell did it mean "make sure everything is fitted correctly"? And charge it?*

A smaller box fell from the outer packaging, hitting Olivia's desk with a thump. *What the hell?*

Kegel balls.

She opened the matte black box and inside were bright pink balls, two of them, with a firm silicon band protruding at an odd angle.

"Seriously?" she said to no one.

Picking up the phone, she replied to the message.

> What do you want me to do with these?

Immediately, Victoria's reply came.

Read the instructions.

Olivia shook her head. What on earth had she let herself in for? And then another message came through from Victoria.

I thought journalists were supposed to be curious?

She stared at the question. *Oh, hell. Really?* What had she let herself in for?

Olivia typed out her reply.

I am, hence my questions.

Then sat back in her chair, holding the implement in her fingers.

All this because she wanted to get closer to Alison. Was this really worth it? She knew what she should do, or at least she should have done weeks ago now. Recuse herself, and hand Alison's therapy to one of her colleagues, but could she? Was she going too far? But she couldn't stop her hands from running over the smooth silicon. Victoria didn't know who she was so did she really have anything to lose?

Chapter 15
ABBY

Abby lay on the bed, the soft padded cuffs around her wrists and ankles secured to the nylon restraints which disappeared under the mattress. Her eyes never left Victoria as her mistress walked around the room, holding the short leather crop in one hand, letting it glance against her other palm. The repeated motion of leather against skin sent goosebumps across Abby's flesh.

Was her punishment to be whipped? If it was, then there was a tiny bit of her that was grateful for her earlier mistake. But then she remembered Victoria's stark warning. This time there would be punishment as recompense for her behaviour, but there would be no next time for any repetition. Abby knew it was no idle threat. When Victoria demanded complete devotion, Abby knew better than to deny her mistress.

"What am I going to do with you?" Victoria stared down at her, her expression stoic, the question rhetorical.

Abby lowered her gaze. It felt brazen to meet her mistress's eyes when punishment was about to be administered.

"I could whip you. Pull your legs apart." Victoria pulled on a nylon restraint and Abby felt her ankles distance themselves even further. A draught tickled her centre, her lips now parted. "Allow the paddle to strike at your very core."

Abby raised her eyebrows, a little shocked. Victoria had only ever whipped her on her buttocks or on the front or back of her thighs, but never…there. She felt sure if her legs hadn't been restrained, she might have involuntarily crossed them. Under hooded eyes, she snuck a glance upwards. Victoria was staring at her centre, which Abby knew must be wet with arousal. As she watched the crop rise into the air, Abby took in a sharp breath, squeezed her eyes shut and braced herself. But rather than the sharp blow she expected, she felt nothing. Easing one eye open, she looked to where the crop had been, only to see empty air, but she jumped as the coolness of the leather gently stroked her ever-swelling clit. A shudder raked its way through her body, willing her mistress to do whatever she desired. Again, the leather caressed her arousal, a little firmer this time, and Abby groaned.

"Did I say you could make a noise?"

Abby swallowed, lowering her eyes and giving the slightest shake of her head. *Fuck, this is hot*, she thought, knowing her wetness was betraying the demure front she was offering. The bed moved and suddenly she felt her mistress's warm breath against her slickness. Victoria was between her legs, and Abby's clit was twitching for attention.

"You'd like nothing more than to have me tease you with my tongue, wouldn't you?"

Warm air swept over her centre, and Abby arched her back, moaning loudly.

"Do you want me to fuck you with my tongue? To ravish you until you beg me to stop?"

"Yes." That was exactly what she wanted, to be taken by

her mistress, to be taught a lesson she would never forget. Her body fought hopelessly against the restraints to raise her hips towards the seduction of Victoria's mouth, but the bed moved again and all it left her with was a sense of loss.

"I didn't give you permission to speak." Victoria stood at the end of the bed. "I'm questioning your devotion, my Pet. I think you need to think hard about your behaviour because I don't accept sloppy subs. When I come back, you'll either tell me you are ready to give me your complete unfaltering devotion, or I'll happily release you from our arrangement."

Abby's jaw fell open. Was Victoria really about to walk away, leaving her wet and throbbing? She opened her mouth to protest, then caught herself. If she wanted her mistress to take her, to own her completely, then she needed to stay silent. As Victoria walked out of the room, it left Abby with one thought: what would it take to show her mistress her utter devotion?

It was the same thought she spent the next ten minutes considering, or it could have been longer. It felt longer. A lot longer. When Victoria eventually reappeared, Abby was appropriately repentant. Resolved to agree, willingly, to whatever demands came her way. She remained silent, not looking directly at the woman she felt fortunate to still call Mistress.

The sound of glass on wood and a faint rustle caught her attention, but she didn't turn her head.

"Well? Have you had sufficient time to consider your behaviour?"

Abby swallowed.

"Do you want me to untie you from the restraints? And look at me when you answer."

Abby glanced up, shaking her head.

"Say it," Victoria commanded.

"No, Mistress." Abby shook her head again. "I want you to

keep me tied up so you can punish me for my unacceptable behaviour."

A slow smile crept over Victoria's face as she lifted the wineglass to her lips. Abby followed a droplet of condensation as it ran from fingertips down the chilled glass.

"You know I'll not let you off easily." Victoria's eyes steadied, holding Abby in her gaze. Abby didn't dare breathe. Lifting her glass above Abby's torso, Victoria tipped the rim towards Abby's stomach with a precise, smooth movement. A finger held an ice cube in place, only allowing a little of the freezing liquid to splash against her skin. Abby swallowed a gasp. No matter what was ahead of her, she would not make a sound. That much she had promised herself. Even when Victoria lowered her mouth to Abby's body, and she felt her mistress's tongue follow the chilled trail with the warm heat of her tongue, she remained silent.

Victoria laughed. Abby knew that from the bullet rigidity of her nipples and the damp patch that lay between her legs, Victoria didn't need to hear her gasps to know the effect she was having.

"What's your safe word, my Pet?" Victoria lifted something from a bag. Abby turned her head to see a candle. Taking the small stiff wick between her fingers and straightening it, Victoria then reached down to where her glass sat and lifted a silver lighter, which Abby had never seen before.

"Fray Bentos, Mistress."

Victoria nodded, taking her time as she brought the flame to the wick. "And do you wish to proceed with your punishment?" Lifting the candle a little higher, Victoria allowed the first drop of hot wax to splash against her own palm. Abby watched as her mistress closed her eyes, obviously enjoying the sensation.

"Yes, please, Mistress."

"Then close your eyes, and don't open them. I don't want you to get…needlessly hurt."

Abby did as instructed. Eyes closed, silent, she waited. The room was quiet. Abby's only sensation came from the slight acrid smell as the wick burned further. She imagined the flame licking the wax, making its surface melt under its touch.

The first drop hit between her breasts. The shock of the burn gave way to a pleasurable heat as it slid down towards her stomach. The second hit a little farther down and was as pleasant, though without the element of surprise it didn't seem as hot.

"Green, amber, red?" Victoria's question hung in the air as Abby breathed deeply.

"Green, Mistress. Definitely, green."

"Then we should increase your level of punishment."

Abby felt the air around her shift slightly. Had her mistress moved positions? The bed remained level, but something was happening… Then the large splash of wax hit her nipple and she couldn't stop the noise from her sharp intake of breath. She was so consumed by the pleasure in the burning tenderness that she didn't hear the high-pitched clink of the ice cube leaving the glass until it made contact with her nipple. The shock of cold upon hot was strangely erotic, made even more so when Victoria's fingers swept lightly over her centre. Then, for a moment, she held completely still. *No,* she thought, *she wouldn't.*

Victoria must have sensed her apprehension because she leant down towards her ear and whispered, "there's no wax going there… I just want to see how well this punishment is hitting the mark."

Abby relaxed—as much as she could in the restraints—allowing her body to sink into the mattress.

"Don't get too comfortable." Her mistress wasted no time

in serving the same punishment to Abby's other breast, moving back and forth until she dripped with desire. Both of her nipples were erect and tight under the cooling wax, but permission hadn't been granted for her to open her eyes, so they remained tight shut. The pressure of her mistress's fingertips over the barely supple wax was pleasantly tender, causing her desire to grow with every pass.

Victoria's voice was soft when she eventually spoke. "We can either remove this quickly or slowly. I say…"

Abby held her breath.

"Quickly." Victoria yanked a piece of the reformed wax from Abby's left nipple, causing her to groan loudly. She had barely caught her breath when the largest piece of wax on her other breast followed suit. Had she not been restrained, she would have wanted to wrap her arms over her tender flesh as her mind lost itself in confusion between pleasure and pain. These were the same sensations she had felt the first time Victoria had spanked or whipped her, but now, as then, she learned that surrender brought peace.

"Open your eyes." Her mistress kissed the bright pink flesh of Abby's breasts, slowly removing the last slivers of wax as she went. As the adrenalin abated, Abby felt a little tearful as she watched the tender care her mistress afforded her. How could she have ever even considered disobeying her mistress? It was a mistake she would never make again. Not ever.

"Mistress?" Abby had tried to hold back, but the words needed to tumble out of her mouth.

"Yes, my Pet?" Victoria continued to kiss her sensitive areola, glancing up to meet Abby's eyes.

"Mistress, I love you."

"I love you too, my Pet, but do I have your complete devotion?"

Abby nodded. "My complete devotion. Mistress, I promise I'll never—"

A single finger placed by her mistress against her lips stopped her from saying anymore.

"I always reward devotion," Victoria whispered before sliding her hand down Abby's body, "and it seems you are more than a little ready."

Abby allowed her head to fall back as Victoria eased herself between her legs. Her mistress's light strokes rendered Abby helpless, but that was nothing compared to the pleasure her mistress unleashed, sucking her into her mouth. Abby lost herself in the euphoria that was her mistress, exhilarated to be exactly where she should be in the world. *Everyone should have a mistress like Victoria*, she thought as the tingle of orgasm overtook her body. As all coherent reasoning slipped away into the oblivion of pleasure, she knew she'd do whatever it took to make Victoria happy.

Chapter 16
ALISON

From the moment Alison arrived home, she knew something had changed. The air was charged and as hard as she tried to get Abby to meet her gaze, the younger woman seemed to look everywhere except at Alison. Her stomach dropped. Abby had told Victoria about what had happened earlier.

Victoria was on her phone, listening intently while pouring herself an enormous glass of wine. A glass far larger than she'd usually have on a school night. Alison shrugged off her coat and went upstairs to change. As soon as she was in the safety of her own room, she closed the door and leant against it, breathing heavily. What had so nearly happened with Abby had been preying on her mind, and the guilt that came with it was swallowing her whole. Knowing that Victoria knew what had transpired, that she had been so close to taking Abby, Victoria's one true love, without her consent, made her more anxious than she had ever felt at the hands of Mhairi.

Mhairi always told Alison what befell her was always by her own doing. Alison had believed her. It was why she had willingly handed over all control. But today she had wanted to be the one in control, and look where that had gotten her.

The knock on her bedroom door made her jump.

"Alison, can I come in?" Victoria's request sent a fresh wave of anxiousness over an already delicate stomach.

She'd rather just go to bed and pull the covers over her head, pretending that none of it had happened. But she knew that wasn't an option. Not just because Victoria wouldn't allow her to hide away, but because she needed to stand up and be accountable for her actions. The last three months of therapy had taught her that much.

"Come in." Backing away from the door, she edged back towards the bed, unsure of what Victoria was about to unleash. Whatever it was, it would only be what she deserved, that much was certain.

"How was your day?" Oddly, the calmness of Victoria's question only served to unnerve Alison even more, if that was possible. Rage would have been easier to deal with. It was a far more familiar response.

"Okay," she mumbled, but unable to cope with any ongoing small talk, she went straight for the enormous elephant which was sitting painting its toenails in the centre of the room. "I know Abby will have told you what I did—what I nearly did—and I need you to know it was entirely my fault. I had Abby in the restraints and there was nothing she could do and I took advantage of—"

"Shall we sit?" Victoria pointed to the bed, which Alison had all but backed into as she edged farther into the room. Alison did as she was told, lowering her gaze. The bed moved as Victoria joined her, and it surprised her to feel the heat of Victoria's thigh against her own.

"Abby has told me what happened, and she, too, claims it was all her doing. Not only was she desperate to take the blame, but she wanted to exonerate you completely, claiming the only reason things didn't cross a line that would have been impossible to have come back from was because of your restraint."

Alison ran her fingers over the thighs of her jeans in a repetitive motion, but didn't speak. She couldn't find the words. It was so like Abby to take the fall for what had happened, and Alison felt ashamed that someone so much younger than her had the integrity she so often lacked. Victoria halted the motion of her fingers against the denim as she grasped her hand. Alison froze. Would her mistress's anger come now?

To her surprise, Victoria lifted her hand and placed a light kiss on her knuckles. Alison looked up at Victoria, her brow wrinkled in question. Victoria was offering her a gentle, almost understanding smile.

"I—" Alison shook her head. Whatever was happening, this didn't come close to any of her expectations. Mhairi would have humiliated her, berated her and psychologically dehumanised her to the point Alison would have crawled on her belly to obtain forgiveness. Victoria was doing none of that.

"I can't even begin to imagine what you have been going through after Mhairi, and I will not insult you by telling you I understand because I don't. Only somebody who has lived through years of toxicity can come close to appreciating the pain. Even then, they will never really understand because no two people experience it in the same way, even if the abuse is identical. What I can tell you is that I am so damned proud of the way you are dealing with what has happened. You have applied yourself to the therapy, opened yourself up to being vulnerable even though I can see the pain it causes you, and have shown bravery beyond all expectation. I love you for all of that and even more for your courage to keep getting up and being open to whatever the healing process brings. I love you for being you."

The lump that formed in Alison's throat made it impossible to breathe, let alone speak. When she opened her mouth, a strangled croak was all that she managed. The warmth of Victoria's other hand on the small of the back offered a reassuring rub. It screamed *I've got you*, leaving Alison with a swirling sensation of relief, safety and disbelief. This was too overwhelming to process.

"But I broke the rules." Her voice was raspy with emotion. "You should throw me to the wolves. It's what I deserve."

Victoria pulled her close, placing her head against her chest. "You didn't break the rules. You exercised restraint, overriding your desire, and with someone as beautiful and innocent as Abby, I know how hard that is to do."

Alison took comfort in feeling Victoria's fingers weaving through her long blonde hair, massaging her scalp.

"Healing is a complex process. You are reclaiming parts of yourself that were lost, abused, and that means taking back your power. It's all about experimenting, and the wonderful thing about experiments is that sometimes you'll get it right and sometimes you'll get it wrong. Today it nearly went very wrong, but it didn't because you stopped yourself. I'd say today was a triumph of sorts."

"I should have never left you," Alison said weakly.

Victoria kissed her forehead.

"The love I feel for you runs deeper than any faux pas which might pass between us, but it doesn't mean things could go back to what had been before. Just as the ground rules have changed for Abby, they have to change for you, too. This is all part of your journey. You outgrew me as your mistress before and you're outgrowing me as your mistress now."

Alison's face was distraught. "No. You can't cast me out. I can't cope. Not yet."

"Nobody is casting you out. Your place is still here, with us for now, but not as my sub. Abby is my sub and always will be. It's where she is happiest and it's where she holds the most control, whether she realises it, or not. But not you."

Confusion clouded Alison's thoughts. If she wasn't Victoria's sub then who was she? It was all she had known for most of her adult life.

"Then where do I belong? If I belong?" Alison's voice shook with obvious fear.

"We are still us, all three of us as lovers, but not as Mistress, Pet and Kitten because that's what you've outgrown. But what we share, we now share as us: Alison, Abby and Victoria. I want you to join us in bed tonight and every night you want to be there, but I won't orchestrate any activities. It'll be three consenting strong women enjoying each other's minds and bodies. I might even enjoy a night off from being in charge." Victoria chuckled.

"But Abby—you said she'd always be your sub?" Alison asked, her head now taking comfort against Victoria's chest.

"True. And that will be between Abby and I. I am her mistress, and she is under no illusions about where her devotions lie. It's probably best if you don't ask her to test out any of your new creations going forward. You don't want to be disappointed when she refuses."

Alison looked up, surprised to see Victoria smiling.

"Were you this understanding with her?" she asked, curious to know what had played out while she had been away.

"Mm. That's the job of being a good mistress. You need to know the best way to apply that understanding. All you need to know is that she has found as much comfort from me as you hopefully have."

Alison looked deep into Victoria's eyes and then, placing her hand around the back of her neck, pulled her down into a deep kiss that seemed to go on forever.

Chapter 17
ALISON

Abby had left at the crack of dawn, racing down the stairs at breakneck speed to meet Matt who had screeched up the driveway and then braked with such force it convinced Alison he was doing a doughnut in the gravel. Victoria just turned over and sighed when she heard the commotion, throwing her arm over Alison's waist and pulling her closer.

The three of them had made love into the early hours of the morning, giving, receiving and sharing the delight of each other's bodies without rules or roles in what Alison could only describe as one of her most liberating sexual experiences.

Her limbs ached with the delicious soft echo of satisfaction, and lying here in Victoria's embrace, being the little spoon, was bliss. She almost wished she could lie like this forever. Almost. But today was Thursday and that meant time with Olivia.

Letting out a long sigh, Alison tried to guess what dress she'd be wearing. Maybe the light coloured one with the tiny daisies, or would it be the black one with the big bright embroidered flowers, or would she be wearing a new one?

"What are you thinking about?" Victoria asked, running her hand over Alison's naked stomach.

"I've a therapy session today. I was just thinking about what we'd talk about."

"With the alluring Dr Hopkins?" Victoria's hand darted down between Alison's legs, giving her a playful tickle.

"Don't start what you can't finish," snapped Alison, pushing Victoria's hand away. "And she's not alluring. We have a professional relationship."

"Whatever you say… I'm making no comment, but it seems to me the woman doth protest too much. Now, snuggle down because we've another hour before the alarm goes off and after last night's activities, we both need our beauty sleep. We don't have the luxury of Abby's youth on our side."

Alison couldn't remember the last time she slept so soundly, and it was only thanks to a full volume alarm that she roused at all. Having given themselves just enough time to shower and run, they'd hardly spoken, but as Alison emerged into the kitchen, she caught the end of a conversation Victoria was having with Gareth.

Quietly she made coffee as they said their goodbyes, but she didn't give Victoria time to draw breath before she asked, "Why was Gareth calling?"

"A Mhairi update. They still haven't located her. All they can tell is that she hasn't attempted to leave the country. More's the pity."

"But how do they know? She might have already gone under another false passport." Alison knew she was clutching at straws, but to be free of Mhairi's irritation would be akin to getting over chickenpox. It was strange how distance and healing made you see things differently. If someone had asked Alison to have drawn a disease comparison a few months ago, she'd have likened Mhairi to rabies, fatal unless you have been inoculated, but even then it would cause you severe distress. But now she was definitely chickenpox, and Alison's scabs were drying up.

"Facial recognition, according to Gareth. Although, ask any of the relevant authorities and they'll claim they don't use it. That's how they tracked her entry. She came in via Roscoff to Cork, travelled up to Northern Ireland and then arrived in Troon. They've still never found the grey Astra with false plates that picked her up or the old, fat, bald guy. He's not known on any of the databases seemingly, although I find that difficult to believe, given the types that Mhairi mixes with."

"She used to mix with me, but I'm not on any databases." Alison shrugged. "Well, I will not stop living my life because they can't locate her. She can't hurt me, and I don't need babysitting."

Victoria grimaced. "Nobody is babysitting you."

Alison raised an eyebrow.

"Look, we both know how dangerous she can be when she gets riled and we both know that the one thing she'll want more than anything else is money. The easiest way to get money out of us is to take one of us and use them as leverage. Most likely it'd be you...or Abby," Victoria said. "If she took Abby, I'd kill her."

"But not me?"

"Of course I'd kill her if she took you. Anyway, we're not going to allow that to happen. It's a moot point." Victoria slipped one arm into her wool coat and then another.

"Look, I can drive myself into the therapy session. I'm perfectly capable," Alison said, trying to keep any hint of a whine out of her voice.

"I'd rather you didn't. Think about my safety. If you go in by yourself, you're leaving me on my own."

"Oh, for god's sake, with the cameras and security gates

and everything else you've got around here, this is like living in Fort Knox. Nothing and no one will get near you."

"I'm still coming," Victoria said.

"Fine, have it your way, but I'm refusing to allow her to dictate what I do in my life." Alison pulled on her jacket, picked up her bag and said, "so are we going then?" Victoria didn't wait.

Victoria elected to drive. They weaved their way through the early morning traffic into Edinburgh.

"I don't want to be late," she said again to Victoria, who simply raised an eyebrow.

"This coming from the woman who'd be late for her own funeral. When have you ever cared about being late for anything?" The amusement in Victoria's voice only irritated Alison further.

By the time they got into town, there were only five minutes to spare before her appointment was due to start.

"I'll just park here. I'll be here when you come out," said Victoria.

"What, you're just going to sit here?"

"Yeah, I've got stuff to do. I can just sit and wait."

"Oh god, it's like having a security guard. What, are you going to watch the door to make sure nobody else comes in?" Alison said petulantly.

"No, I'm going to do some work. Go and enjoy." Victoria waved her off, pushing back the driver's seat in the Defender and stretching out her legs.

Chapter 18
VICTORIA

It was amusing seeing Alison so flustered. The fact that she had a crush on her therapist was clear, although if Victoria was to ask her outright, she'd probably deny it. Desperate to be uncharacteristically on time wasn't the only clue; she had dressed a little smarter and was even wearing makeup, Victoria noted. All things Alison didn't do regularly. But Victoria's levity this morning wasn't just coming from Alison and her crush. No, she had her trainee to think about. Pulling out her phone, she scrolled through her contacts until she found the name she was looking for, 'Kerry Patterson'. With a wicked grin, she tapped out a text message.

I hope you've done as you were told?

Pushing the button to lower the back of the driver's seat, just a tad, Victoria settled in and waited for a reply. In a flash, the response came back.

I have. I'm a little nervous.

> Good girl. Now I want you to sit back and
> enjoy.

> What are you going to do?

Victoria could almost hear the woman's anxiety as she read the message.

> I'm going to have some fun and you're going
> to do exactly as you're told. Here are this
> morning's rules. You will carry on as if
> nothing is happening.

Victoria had barely hit the send button before the vibration told her she had a new message from Kerry.

> I have meetings!

Victoria looked at her phone and gave a slight frown. Perhaps this woman would not be as easy to train as she'd initially thought.

> You can still play.

Then she immediately followed it up with a more terse response. She didn't have the time or inclination to waste on somebody who wasn't serious.

> You either do this my way or not at all.

She hit send and then relaxed back into the seat, closing her eyes. The choice the other woman made would not impact her day, and after all, that was the important factor: choice. Her phone burst into life, and she rolled her eyes behind closed lids. Before looking at the screen, she knew who it would be.

"Yes," Victoria said, holding the phone to her ear.

"I have meetings this morning. I can't just cancel my day."

"First, you will address me as Mistress."

"I-I," the voice at the end of the line stuttered.

"Second, I am not asking you to cancel your meetings. Quite the opposite."

The woman didn't say a word.

"You will carry on your day as normal and whatever I choose to do, you will accept. What I will tell you is that under no circumstances can you touch yourself, or have anyone else satisfy your needs. Do I make myself clear?" There was an audible gulp at the end of the line. "Do I make myself clear?" Victoria repeated.

"Yes, Mistress," came the reply.

"If you do, I will find out." And then she cut the call and pulled up the app on her phone. *Let the vibrations begin*, she thought with a smile.

When she'd told Abby what she was planning to do, Abby was shocked, but Victoria could tell that she was in equal part fascinated. Victoria explained that once the Kegel balls were in place, she could then control them via an app on her phone…whenever she wanted. The way that Abby's eyes lit up at the thought of being so utterly submissive made Victoria realise she'd have to pick up another set from the warehouse today.

Having two women vibrating at the touch of a fingertip was an entertaining idea…

Chapter 19
ALISON

A quick check of her watch and Alison saw her therapist was running a good fifteen minutes late. She glanced over to the older lady sitting behind the reception desk with her cropped grey hair. She looked like a formidable character and returned Alison's gaze with an air of disgust. But Alison didn't take it personally; the woman seemed to have the same dislike for everybody that walked in. That was until a tall blond-haired man in his forties swept his way through into the reception.

"Mr Lawson," the woman behind the reception said. "How nice to see you again, twice in one week. You're spoiling us."

The chap stopped, looked at her, cocked his head and said, "Okay." He seemed confused by the receptionist's pleasure in seeing him. "Can you give this to Olivia, please? She left it at the flat and she'll need it. It's getting cold."

He took a thick tartan scarf from his pocket. It looked expensive, Alison thought, as she watched their exchange.

"Of course," said the receptionist. "I'll make sure she gets it."

"Thank you." Turning on his heel, he left the office. He was like one of those old-fashioned hovercrafts her parents had taken her on when they went on holiday to the Isle of Wight; he inflated and then glided across the polished wooden floor effortlessly. Alison glanced back at the receptionist, who was now looking a little flushed and *smiling*. Then it occurred to Alison, the receptionist only smiled at men. Alison cringed. Women like this put feminism back decades, but the woman's smile was quickly replaced as she stared at her screen, and then Alison.

"Dr Hopkins will see you now," she said, more with a sneer, and Alison was glad to leave her company.

She was equally glad when she got into the office and realised that Olivia had chosen not to sit behind her desk today, but at the two large armchairs next to the fireplace. It wasn't lit and Alison doubted it was even in working order anymore, but still the large black grate and Victorian tiles made an impressive centrepiece to the room. It also gave their session a sense of intimacy.

"What's her problem?" Alison asked as she dropped into the worn, saggy cushion, nodding towards the reception.

"Whose problem?" Olivia asked.

"Your receptionist rottweiler."

"Sharon?"

"Yeah. She gives everybody else the death stare but in walks a man and she's like, oooh."

Olivia smiled. "Sharon is a bit of an acquired taste."

"Like marzipan?"

Olivia gave a light laugh, and Alison couldn't help but think it was one of the most beautiful sounds she'd ever heard.

"I was thinking of something a touch more acidic." Olivia shook her head. "I shouldn't say that. Sharon works very hard for us."

"She looked at me as though I was something she'd trodden in, then in walks this blonde chap, granted he was quite good looking—oh, he brought in a scarf for you, I think —but anyway, she was beside herself, fawning over him."

Olivia nodded. "Hmm."

Alison wanted to ask who it was because where did she leave her scarf? She *really* wanted to know the answer. "Yeah, so it looks like you've got competition for your man," she said with a smile.

Olivia's eyes widened. "Competi— No, no, absolutely not. It would have been Lucas. He's my ex-husband. And ex for a long time."

Alison drew her head back. "But you still pop round?"

Olivia seemed confused. "Exactly what was the conversation that I missed?"

"Oh, he just brought in a scarf and said you'd left it the last time you were round."

Olivia looked dumbfounded. "We're still friends. We vaguely keep in touch. Anyway, enough about me. This is your session. Tell me what's happening with Mhairi. That was quite a thunderbolt that you left on last time. I've been thinking about it all week."

Alison grinned. "You've been thinking about me all week?"

Olivia rolled her eyes. "I've been thinking about your situation. You are incorrigible."

"I'm absolutely fine. We haven't heard any more, we don't know where she is. I'm quite relaxed about the whole thing. I don't think she's going to come after me. Victoria is…slightly more concerned. She keeps thinking everybody is about to jump out of a bush and abduct us, but I refuse to change what I'm doing. Besides, I feel stronger now, and I keep having this daydream, fantasy thing, where I get to confront her. It's quite empowering."

"Empowering?" Olivia's brows knitted together, urging Alison to explain.

"Oh, it's…she confronts me and I take her down. Simple as that, really."

"That doesn't sound simple to me at all," said Olivia. "So you fight her?"

"Well, more or less, yeah. I kick her arse, and there's something so satisfying about it. And there's also something…I don't know. Sexual about it."

"This you need to explain," Olivia said.

But Alison didn't see the usual glint in her eye she usually had when they talked talked about sex. This was different. There was genuine concern reflected in her expression.

Alison said, "Well, it's not about me having sex with Mhairi. It's having so much power, it's…I don't know… exhilarating. Anytime I've been on my own and I've had this fantasy about kicking Mhairi's arse, or even just getting the opportunity to do it, I feel turned on. Is that normal?"

"I've yet to find a satisfactory definition of the word normal. But it's certainly interesting. Why do you think you're having these fantasies and the sexual response?" Olivia asked.

Alison looked at her and she said, "well, I think you and I know why that is. I'm healing, I'm getting stronger."

Olivia nodded, the hint of a smile playing on her lips. "And as you get stronger, how does that affect your relationship with Victoria and Abby?"

Alison narrowed her eyes. Olivia had an uncanny ability to ask questions that jabbed at whatever was hurting, even though Alison had never told her about any issues. But before she could answer, Olivia gave a slight jump.

"Are you okay?" Alison asked her.

"Yes, s-sorry."

Alison watched as she crossed and uncrossed her legs again, almost grinding down into the chair.

Her eyebrows shot up and then when she spoke, it was in a much higher octave than it had been before. "Carry on, you were telling me about Victoria and Abby."

Alison nodded and surveyed her therapist, wondering just what was going on. Something wasn't right, but Olivia obviously didn't want to talk about it, or at least not to Alison.

"We're having to navigate it as we go." Alison wasn't ready to talk about the fact Victoria was no longer her mistress because it still held a twinge of pain that she wasn't able to articulate. "Their bond is more intense than I have with either of them, and I want to find somebody I connect with in the same sort of way, but preferably somebody who hasn't got a husband or another lover."

"It…right, yes, yes."

Alison stopped and just stared at Olivia. Whatever was happening to her therapist seemed to have quite an impact. Olivia's cheeks were flushed, and she fidgeted in a way that suggested it aroused her, as though she was on the verge of— *No, surely not.* Alison couldn't take her eyes off her.

"Olivia, do you want to talk about what you're feeling right now?"

"No! I would appreciate it if you call me Dr Hopkins." Olivia's voice hitched, and she squirmed in the large armchair.

Alison laughed. "Okay, Dr Hopkins. But if you're in some sort of—distress, maybe we should talk about it."

"Alison, this is your therapy session," said Olivia, appearing to regain a little control. "We should concentrate on you, but—we only appear to have five minutes left, so I suggest you make the most of that time."

Alison shrugged. "Maybe I should tell you that I had

multiple orgasms last night at both Victoria and Abby's hands—and mouths," she grinned, "and none of them involved any form of submission." By the time Alison had finished her sentence, her face was poker straight.

"Alison, for you that's groundbreaking. And typically you wait until the very end of the session to offer the most significant topic for discussion." Olivia's eyes suddenly grew wilder and Alison was pretty sure it had little to do with her revelation. Instead of poising her pen over the pad as she normally did, the therapist had both hands clutched tightly onto the arms of the chair she sat in.

When Alison mentioned her use of a strap-on as Abby sat astride her, she was sure she heard her therapist whimper.

"I'm sorry. I'm going to have to stop you there. Our time is up."

Alison fell silent. No session had ever ended as abruptly before. Olivia usually got up, shook her hand and opened the door for her, but not today. The woman was glued to the seat.

"I think you can, um, see, um, your way out," she said, stammering.

"Okay." Alison got up and grabbed her jacket and bag. "Dr Hopkins, I hope you feel better soon. Your face is looking rather flushed."

Chapter 20
DR OLIVIA HOPKINS

Olivia didn't dare move because the slightest twitch in the wrong direction and she was liable to explode into orgasm. As the door closed behind Alison, Olivia's phone vibrated on her desk. Just by the sound, she knew it was a text message, and she could bloody well guess who it was from.

With a deep breath, she tightened her pelvic floor and tried to stand. Her legs shook. God, what had that woman been trying to do to her? Even as she walked across to her desk, the balls inside her quivered again and she actually let out a small scream. The door to her room threw open, and Sharon stuck her head in.

"Are you all right, Dr Hopkins?"

Olivia froze on the spot. "Yes," she said, her voice quivering almost as much as her legs. "I'm fine. If you could just go out, I have some notes to write up."

Sharon looked at her quizzically. "Can I get you a glass of water?"

"No, Sharon. I don't want anything except a little peace and quiet. If you don't mind?"

The older woman frowned, obviously not appreciating

the tone with which she was being addressed, but Olivia had neither the control nor the will to care. Grabbing the desk with both hands, she widened her stance, ready for the next round of vibrations, unsure if her body could take anymore. Until today, she had no idea her body could feel like this.

Taking a deep breath, she lifted her phone, and sure enough, there was a message from Victoria.

> Good girl. I'm very proud of you. You have the makings of a good little sub. Relax for the rest of the day and we can play again tomorrow. Then you can tell me how much you enjoyed it.

Olivia stared at her phone. Enjoyed it? For the last hour she had sat opposite the woman she'd been obsessing over—sexually obsessing—with vibrating balls inside her. And then the little pink arm kept vibrating against her clitoris. She'd been ready to explode. At one point, when Alison leant forward, her top gaping at the front, Olivia thought she was going to come completely undone. By the end, it was all she could do to get the woman out of the room so she could try to regain some semblance of dignity. She would need to speak to Victoria. This couldn't happen again.

True to Victoria's word, there were no further vibrations for the rest of day and, much to Olivia's surprise, she enjoyed the movement of the weights inside her, offering the glow of arousal throughout the day. Had she had a partner to go home to, it would have proved to have been an interesting evening. But sadly it was Olivia on her own, sitting on her sofa, focusing on her spag bol for one, in an attempt to keep her hands busy.

Eventually, having eaten and unable to focus on anything but her arousal, she picked up the phone and called Victoria. The phone rang three times before it was answered.

"Good evening." The voice was assured but warm. "I trust you had a good day," Victoria said.

"Well, that's what I need to talk to you about." There was a quaver in Olivia's voice, but she had to say this. "I'm afraid I don't think that this is a very good idea."

Victoria sounded surprised. "Really?"

"Perhaps if we could just do this within certain hours?"

"Uh, have I got this wrong or did you want to learn to be a domme?"

"Yes, yes. But-but this isn't what I had in mind."

"And didn't I explain to you that in order to be a domme, you had to be a good sub first? How can you give orders when you don't know how to take orders?"

"Yes, I understand that, but—"

"Then you will listen to what I'm about to say."

"I—"

"You will listen." Victoria's voice took on an authoritative tone. "I want you to assign a ringtone, a very specific one that's only used for me, and when you hear that ringtone, I want you to follow the command you are given—immediately. Do you understand?"

"But I don't know—"

"Do you understand?" Victoria cut across her.

Reluctantly, Olivia agreed, still bemused how this call had gone from her determination to assert herself, into her agreeing to whatever was demanded of her, no matter where she might be. All in the pursuit of Alison. Approaching Victoria had been done, intending to learn how to make Alison happy, because that's what she really wanted to understand. How to sexually satisfy Alison had been the goal just on the off chance she might get that opportunity, but every encounter with Victoria seemed to take her farther away from that aim, not closer. And yet, she didn't put a stop to what she had set in motion, rather she capitulated, offering more and more of herself.

With the call ended, she did as she was told and assigned a ringtone to her virtual mistress. "Oh, Fortuna" was the tone she selected as it reflected what happened to her body every time Victoria called.

Chapter 21
VICTORIA

Victoria stood in front of the kitchen counter and slid the button on the app to the right with her forefinger, watching the intensity rating increase.

"Are you playing with her again?" Abby asked, coming up behind her and sliding her arms around her waist.

"Oh, yes. I rang her, then put down the phone before she answered, then sent her a message telling her to find somewhere comfortable and on her own. I'll do this for another day and then I'll stop sending the message, so the only notice she'll get will be the ringtone."

Abby's hands snaked up Victoria's body until she took the weight of her breasts in her hands. "How very Pavlovian."

"Mm, isn't it just?" Victoria groaned as Abby tweaked her nipples. "And so far, she hasn't refused any of my commands."

"Did you expect her to?" Abby asked, pushing her body closer to Victoria.

"Honestly, yes. I thought I'd have had extreme push back by now, but not once has she refused me. I've never had a trainee who was so compliant."

Abby ran her hands down her mistress's sides until she reached the hem of her skirt. "Mistress, may I?" she asked.

"You may." Victoria continued to fiddle with her phone.

"Oh." Abby let out a gasp as she raised her mistress's skirt up her thighs to reveal small lace briefs. "Have you— Ooh, yes, you have."

Victoria chuckled. "Just because you want to take me from behind doesn't mean I have to relinquish control, my Pet." Sliding the intensity a little higher, Victoria took pleasure from the gasps of excitement she was eliciting from her lover; she couldn't believe it had taken her this long to introduce Abby to the toy.

The shaking of Abby's hands as she pulled Victoria's underwear down and ran her fingers through her mistress's slick readiness told her the vibrations were having the desired effect. Abby's fingers slid inside and a hand roughly pushed Victoria forward over the kitchen counter. There was no slow seduction happening here tonight. It was rough and wanton, exactly what Victoria wanted. Widening her stance, she gave Abby the opportunity to go deeper, and she did.

"Harder," Victoria demanded. "Harder still, and I'll give you more pleasure."

Abby thrust deep inside, reaching around at the same time to stroke Victoria's clit, not breaking her tempo even when Victoria, through groans of her own, increased the vibrational intensity of the Kegel balls.

"Do you think now might be the time to see how my trainee is getting on?" Victoria panted.

"Fuck. You wouldn't, would you?" Abby gasped.

They were both panting, on the edge of orgasm, and nobody was more relieved than Victoria when Abby said she wouldn't be able to hold off long enough for the call to be made. Instead, she requested her mistress's permission to come, and Victoria, who had not been sure how much longer she was going to hold out—there was no way she was going to give in first—was glad to give Abby what she wanted.

"Yes, come," Victoria ordered, and the two of them came together in a series of anguished moans. Abby clung to Victoria as she tried to calm her breathing down and her mistress did not move. Victoria loved these spontaneous moments when they gave in to desire, and the new toy seemed to make these encounters more frequent.

Finally, legs still shaky, they made their way to the sofa, and Abby curled into her mistress. Victoria ran her fingers through Abby's hair as she felt the warmth of her lover against her chest. In these moments, she couldn't have felt more aligned, more connected to Abby than she already was.

But she had a call to make.

"I need to call her." Victoria lifted her phone and scrolled until she found the number.

"Oh god, I forgot about her. Will she be alright?"

Victoria shrugged. "We're about to find out."

A panting voice answered. "Yes?"

"And how is your evening?" Victoria asked.

"You have to stop this. You have to let me come."

Victoria couldn't deny that she enjoyed hearing her begging. There really was something exhilarating about that power. "I'll tell you when you can come and you're not ready yet."

Abby looked up, eyes wide.

"No, there's, uh…" A strangled noise came from the woman and Victoria knew she had to put her foot down.

"Are you listening to me? I will tell you when you can come and I am not giving that order just now." Victoria tapped her phone again and increased the vibrations.

"I'm taking this out," the voice at the other end of the line panted.

There was noise, but Victoria wasn't sure what was happening. And then it became clear; the woman was indeed removing the Kegel balls. Evidently, she thought she'd found her limit. But Victoria knew that teaching someone to surrender only started when they took the step beyond the limits they imagined for themselves into freedom beyond anything they'd yet known.

Her trainee thought she had reached the very edge of her capabilities, but Victoria knew the woman was only on step one. But before Victoria could say anything else, she was subject to a tirade from the woman she'd called.

"This is ritual humiliation. That's all this is. I didn't ask for this. I didn't sign up for this."

Victoria took a breath and said, "Well, you didn't sign up for anything, you asked for this and if you no longer wish to learn how to be a good domme, then we can end this here. And please don't return the Kegel balls."

"I wanted to learn how to be a domme," the woman at the end of the line said forcefully. "Jenny said you were the best person to teach me. It appears she was wrong."

Victoria counted to ten. Who the hell was this woman to talk to her in this way? Although when she sat back and thought about it for a moment, it was mildly amusing. The woman had been on the edge of orgasm about five times that day, and not once had Victoria allowed her to actually come.

"I wanted to learn to be a domme."

"And I'm teaching you," said Victoria.

"You're not. You're not teaching me anything. You're teaching me how to humiliate myself and that's it."

Victoria drew in a breath and simply said, "I think this arrangement has come to its natural conclusion. I'd be grateful if you could cease all communications."

But rather than hearing the call end, Victoria held on,

listening to pleas from the woman who only moments earlier was berating her.

"No, I just need you to teach me to be a domme. I need you to—" But the woman didn't finish what she had started.

How ironic, Victoria thought. The specifics of what was driving this woman's needs were still something she found difficult to articulate, or was she just unwilling to share that information with her?

"I don't think so," said Victoria. "To be a good domme, you need to be a good sub, and right now you are not a good sub. Nobody talks to me, their mistress, like this." And with that, she ended the call.

Calmly, she handed the phone to Abby, who placed it down on the coffee table in front of them, knowing what would happen next. The only question would be how long it would take.

Sure enough, within a minute her phone sprang into life and, lo-and-behold, it was her trainee. Victoria had her exactly where she wanted her and after this next round was where her training would really begin.

"Aren't you going to answer it?" Abby asked.

"No, darling. We'll just have a relaxing evening together. Why don't you find something for us to watch and I'll open a bottle of wine?"

The phone continued to ring.

"Abby, darling, can you pop that on silent for me?"

They settled down to watch a film, with Victoria refusing to acknowledge the small vibrations emanating from the coffee table. Her trainee was learning a very valuable lesson.

It was only after they'd finished watching the film and Victoria had popped into the kitchen to refill their wine glasses that Abby said, "You need to talk to her."

But Victoria had no intention of folding yet. "If you're so concerned, you answer it."

And Abby did just that. The phone lit up, indicating an incoming call, and she lifted it. Before she could even speak, all she heard was a woman begging, crying, for Victoria to speak to her.

Abby looked desperately at her mistress. "She's…she's not here just now," she stammered.

Victoria shook her head.

"Give me the phone." Victoria held out her hand to take the phone from Abby who was mouthing a silent, *Sorry.*

"Yes?"

"I'm sorry." Victoria heard the choke of a sob from the woman. "I've put them back in."

"If you think I want to humiliate you or undermine you, then I'm afraid I'm not the person to teach you. This can only work on honesty and respect, so when you're ready to take that step, call me. But not before. Olivia, I don't expect to hear from you again tonight, understood?"

"Yes, but—how do you know my name?"

"Let's leave that discussion for a time when you're ready to open up, shall we?"

Chapter 22
ALISON

Alison sat at the kitchen island, one hand wrapped around a steaming mug of coffee, the other poised over her phone with an outstretched finger scrolling through the BBC News app. Reading the news over coffee was how she started most mornings, but since Gareth's call warning them of Mhairi's UK arrival, she'd been checking local news a little more religiously, and not just in the morning, but throughout the day. A tiny glimmer of hope ignited in her chest every time she scanned through headlines, almost willing the words, "Britain's most evil woman cannot flee justice", or something similar to appear on the page. But just like yesterday and all the days before, there was no such declaration. The reality, Alison knew, was that if Mhairi had been arrested, Gareth would have let Victoria know, but still she looked forward to the day she could read the words.

Until then, she really needed to break this obsessive routine of headline scrolling, and today was going to be the first step to achieving that. Lifting her hand to her head, she allowed her fingers to glide over the short soft fuzz where her long blonde locks had been. The top was longer, and the four inches of blonde hair flopped over her eyes. But the velvet softness of the sides was something she couldn't stop playing with. There was something oddly empowering but equally comforting in the novelty of the touch. For years she'd wanted to cut her hair, mainly because she wanted to return to the early morning swims she'd enjoyed while at college, but Mhairi had always said no. Sitting in the safety of the home she shared with Victoria and Abby, it seemed ridiculous that anyone could have dictated how she looked. But today was a world away from life with Mhairi.

Abby had looked horrified when Alison had told her she'd been forbidden to cut her hair, and even more stricken when she confessed to the fasting regime which Mhairi had enforced upon her.

"But how did she stop you?" she'd asked with an innocence which made Alison's heart ache. It had happened in such small steps that Alison couldn't pinpoint a day or time when things changed. Rather, a series of tiny increments had stripped her of choice, free thought, and most of all, dignity. At first it had been innocuous things, suggestions almost, such as how much Mhairi loved her blonde waves. *Oh don't cut it, pretty please*, she'd said, but that soon turned into a preference, and then an order. The same with Alison's friends. *Do you really want to spend time with them? They're so boring!* morphed into, *They're just using you for your money,* before becoming a direct order of, *I don't want you to see them.* Of course, Alison wanted to keep her mistress happy, so she'd submitted to every request. The only people who were left at the end were Mhairi's friends and Victoria. *Thank god for Victoria*, she thought.

Victoria had been there through it all, and even though Alison tried to hide much of what was happening, more out of shame than anything else, Victoria had simply let her know that whatever Alison chose to do, she'd be by her side.

Mhairi hated her for it, but given Victoria was the financial brains behind their business, and Mhairi loved money (way more than people and, perhaps, even power), she viewed Alison's business partner as a necessary evil. Victoria thought Mhairi was simply evil.

This morning would be the first time she'd realise the benefit of her new style, and she glanced at her watch. In just over an hour, when the tide was high, she'd be meeting her new friends at the swimming club for a dip in the Forth at Ronald Rae, out past Cramond. Wild swimming seemed far more appropriate now than heading to the blandness of a pool.

There had been a morning when she'd tiptoed out into the river's edge, to where it met their land, but the water was murky, and the ground so gloopy it formed suction cups around her feet. Once had been enough, and besides, by joining this group she was meeting new friends, something which Victoria supported.

Just out past the stone fish at Cramond, the beach was firmer, but given the tide could strengthen depending on the season and weather, it was safer to swim with others. This morning it was glorious, and she looked forward to the freedom of swimming in the Forth, as well as the luxury of being able to towel her hair dry, shove on a bit of product and leave it alone. Bringing the coffee cup to her lips, she allowed herself a self-satisfied grin. She felt and looked good with the new 'do' and dressed in deep blue oversized overalls.

Victoria walked in, muttering a "morning" before immediately making her way over to the coffee machine. Pouring herself a large mug, she lifted the pot and with a "want one?" head nod, offered to fill Alison's mug.

Alison shook her head. "No, I'm fine, thanks." The last thing she wanted was to have too much liquid sloshing about in her stomach.

"Well, aren't we just Rosie the Riveter this morning," said Victoria with a laugh. "I love the hair. It looks great. In fact, I love the whole look. It reminds me of when I first met you. The paint-splattered overalls and hair piled on top of your head. I like it short, it's very you. Are you working from your studio today?"

Alison nodded, picking up her coffee cup in two hands. "I will be. Off swimming first and then back to start a new project."

Victoria nodded. "Good. Abby's working from home, too."

Alison understood what Victoria was asking of her without coming straight out and asking. *Stay together, it's safer,* was what *Good* really meant.

"I'm heading into Edinburgh. I'm meeting with the lawyers to complete the purchase of the club. Another six weeks and we should have the keys, but hopefully they'll allow us access so I can get the architects and contractors to start drawing up plans and arranging quotes."

Alison nodded.

"We'll need some bespoke pieces for the place when it's finished, so if you can set some time aside?" Victoria raised her eyebrow. "I know how busy your diary gets. And nothing too risque… We're going after the wedding market with this place, and not just functions, so something classy would be good."

"I've got a few things in mind," Alison said, but all elaboration was curtailed as Abby rushed through the door at breakneck speed, sliding across the tiles.

"Guess what's arrived!" she shouted.

Victoria looked at her and then towards the long hall. "Did you leave the front door open?" she asked.

"What?" Abby frowned.

"Did you leave the front door open? Were you born in a field?" Victoria gestured towards the hall.

"It doesn't matter. I'll get it in a minute. Look what's arrived." Abby triumphantly waved aloft the latest issue of *Darkness*. "Bryce has used nearly everything I sent him. Well, at least his creative director has." Flipping through the pages, she opened it up at the centre and laid it down on the island between where Alison sat and Victoria, who was still by the coffee machine.

Alison peered over, looking at the upside-down image, and then slid off her stool to move around next to Abby. Victoria, coffee cup in hand, moved around to the other side of Abby.

"Wow," she said. "That's quite a shot."

"Isn't it just?" Abby was brimming with enthusiasm.

"Oh, my," said Alison, looking at the centrefold of the magazine, where she was sitting, legs wide, with Abby's head peeking over her thigh. Victoria stood behind them, whip in hand. Then she noticed the welt marks on Abby's cheeks. "Wow," she added.

But Victoria was the one who grabbed the magazine, screwing up her face to look at the smaller image in the bottom right-hand corner. "Abby, what's this?"

Abby took the magazine from her mistress and closed it. "Start with it closed and flick through the pages. Don't take your eyes off the right-hand corner."

Victoria followed Abby's instructions, allowing the pages to flick past her thumb in quick succession. "Oh, my god, Abby, what've you done?"

"Oh, do it faster. The faster you flick, the better it gets," Abby said in a rush, not actually taking in Victoria's shocked expression.

"What is it?" Alison asked.

"See for yourself," Victoria said, handing over the publication.

"What do I do?" Alison asked.

"Go to the front page, go to the bottom, and then start flicking through the pages. But do it fast and you'll see."

Alison did as she was told, and her jaw dropped. Abby, along with Bryce and his creative director, had created a little flick book of the scene Abby had filmed. The three of them were in full action: Victoria was whipping Abby, and Abby was getting to grips with the very core of Alison, who was in the midst of orgasm.

Alison blurted out laughter, but Victoria's expression never moved from one of shock. "I wish you'd told me you were going to do that."

"Don't you think it's great?" Abby said with such enthusiasm it sent Alison into a fit of giggles. The young woman was oblivious to Victoria's unease.

"Mm."

Abby's phone pinged, and she pulled it out of her back pocket.

"It's Matt," she announced, and then, reading his message, she let out a peel of laughter, holding out her phone to let Victoria and Alison read it.

> Omg. You're so hot. What happened? I think I might be on the turn.

Then her phone pinged again, and it was Matt once more.

> We need to celebrate!

Abby held the phone up again, allowing them to read Matt's suggestion.

"He's right. We do need to celebrate. We should have a party," Abby said enthusiastically.

Victoria paled and looked towards Alison with a concerned expression. Alison knew exactly what she was thinking. *Would she be able to cope with a party after what happened before?* But that seemed like a lifetime ago, or at least it did on a good day, and thankfully there were far more good days than bad lately.

"Seems like a good idea to me," Alison said with a shrug

"Are you sure?" asked Victoria. "Don't you think it's a little soon?"

Alison gave her a reassuring smile. It was sweet of Victoria to worry about her, but really, she was in a much better place. The last party they'd all been at ended in the most horrific way possible, but hours of therapy combined with support from both Victoria and Abby meant she was in a stronger position now than she'd been in for years.

"I think a party might be what we all need and besides, I love a good party. Abby and I can work together to organise it," Alison said with a smile that projected the confidence she had started feeling on the inside.

"Okay." Victoria was still nervous, that was obvious from the wariness in her eyes. "I think we should sit down together and perhaps work out some ground rules, though? Maybe keep it all a little tamer than the ones—" She stopped herself.

"You can say it. I won't break. Tamer than Mhairi's parties." Alison pursed her lips, then continued. "But yeah, tamer would be good."

But Abby was ahead of them all, announcing, "The house in Aberdour is free from the seventeenth of December through the twentieth, and then you've got the Christmas booking. That's three full days we can use. We could absolutely have a Christmas party then."

"We're not having a three-day party," Victoria said,

looking horrified at the mere thought, causing both Alison and Abby to exchange amused glances.

"I was thinking more of a day for prep, then a party and that then leaves us a day for clean-up?" Abby was trying to suppress a giggle. "We know you don't have the stamina for a three-dayer... not at your age."

Abby ducked as Victoria lobbed an oven glove in her direction. "We'll see which of the three of us has less stamina tonight," Victoria promised with a glint in her eye.

Alison watched them, happy to be sharing the moment. Lifting a hand to the soft fuzz of hair running up the back of her head, she nodded to herself. She was ready for a party.

Chapter 23
DR OLIVIA HOPKINS

Olivia was sitting in the large high-backed armchair at the side of the fireplace when Alison swept into the room. Her smile was radiant, and it quite took Olivia's breath away, almost as much as the new haircut that she was sporting. Over the last few weeks she had seen a transformation in Alison that not only made her swell with pride, but made the already alluring woman even more attractive. Gone was the nervousness and awkward demeanour she'd carried with her into the initial therapy sessions. Instead, little by little, it had been replaced with a beautifully balanced mix of confidence and a tangible sense of self, not to mention self-worth. Alison was coming into her own.

Olivia rose to her feet to greet her. "You look amazing."

"I feel amazing," said Alison, her broad smile going from ear to ear.

"And your hair." Olivia held out her hands, raising her palms towards Alison's new haircut. "It really suits you. You look like a completely different woman."

"I can't stop touching it." Alison chuckled. "I can't get over how something as simple as a haircut can make me feel so—different. Feel how soft it is." Alison turned her head to the side, inviting Olivia's hand to stroke the short hair.

Reaching out, Olivia let out a girlish laugh and an appreciative *ooh* as her fingertips played with the sensitive skin of Alison's scalp.

"My transformation is thanks to you," she mumbled, placing her hand over Olivia's fingers as though she didn't want her to break contact. For several seconds they just stood, eyes locked on the other, lips inches apart.

"No," said Olivia, reluctantly pulling her hand away. "You've done the hard work. I was just lucky enough to be here to see it happen. You look so happy. It's wonderful. So, talk to me about your happiness." She pointed towards the seat. "Sit down, and tell me everything," she said, taking the chair opposite.

Alison waxed lyrical about wild swimming and the new friends that she'd made, all of which she claimed originated from the decision to cut her hair. A haircut she'd aspired to for years but had never felt enfranchised to get, but now all of that was different. Mhairi was gone. These were choices she was entitled to make, and she revelled in that liberty.

"I feel empowered," said Alison with a cheeky grin. "Like I could take on the world. There's nothing I can't do."

Olivia raised her eyebrows, still smiling. "Nothing?"

"Well, almost nothing," said Alison, and Olivia watched as a veil of thoughts momentarily darkened her features.

"Talk to me about the almost…"

"I need to take accountability for what I want, and that starts at home. With Victoria—and with Abby." Alison took a breath, but she didn't fidget with her cuffs as Olivia had seen her do before. It had been one of her many tells that Olivia had recorded as part of their sessions. A behavioural leakage of anxiety. But today Olivia saw none of that in her client.

"A magazine arrived this morning. I don't know if you've ever heard of it. It's called *Darkness*." Alison paused as if waiting for a glimmer of recognition in Olivia's face, but Olivia simply shook her head. It wasn't anything she'd read. "It's a fetish, BDSM thing," Alison explained.

"Oh," said Olivia. "No, I-I haven't, sorry," she stammered, blushing and shaking her head, embarrassed by being unable to mask her reaction. Silently, she cursed her ineptitude. How could she have ever imagined being a domme that Alison would have respected? The entire idea seemed ridiculous now.

"Don't be sorry, it's quite niche," Alison assured her. "We were in the centrefold, all three of us: Victoria, Abby and myself. We looked awesome. But—" Alison inhaled deeply.

"But?" Olivia would tease this out of Alison no matter what.

"But the whole article is about the three of us being a ménage à trois. It centres on the whole poly thing and well, I'm not sure that's really where I see myself going forward." Alison offered a lopsided smile, a glimpse at the guilt she was harbouring.

"You're still with them, aren't you?" Olivia asked.

"Oh yeah, I'm still with them. For now." Alison met her eyes.

Olivia wasn't sure what to make of it. "Are you about to make some decisions, Alison?"

Alison gave a slow, measured nod. "I think it's time." Pressing her back against the back of the armchair, her eyes scanned the cornice in the room.

Olivia could tell she was searching her soul for answers, and this was a process she would not interrupt. There were moments in the therapeutic journey where silence was the most constructive tool available, and this was one such moment. Eventually, Alison brought her gaze back to Olivia as she assembled her thoughts into words.

"It's a huge coup for Abby and the entire article was funny and bold and very us, but—Bryce had been speaking to Abby about doing more on the three of us and our relationship and I felt so disingenuous. I can't be part of a series that'll come out six months down the line if I don't know if I'll be with them then. What if I've found my person by then?"

Olivia held her breath for a moment, her mind racing between her own wants and desires and that of her client. There was nothing she wanted more than to be that person for Alison, but if her tutelage under Victoria had taught her anything it was that her natural leaning was more towards submissive than dominant, and the release of surrender brought her a depth of solace she hadn't known was achievable. There was one burning question Olivia desperately wanted to know the answer to for many reasons and none of them were professional, but she couldn't stop herself from asking.

"Do you think you've found your person?"

Alison steadied her gaze on Olivia, pinning her to the seat. Olivia heard herself gulp, frightened to even blink.

"I've found somebody I'd like to know better."

Olivia couldn't tear her eyes away from Alison's lips as she said the words, and her heart dropped as she absorbed the confession. Alison was already moving on, ready to pursue someone new, and she had never mentioned this woman once during all their sessions. Olivia cursed herself for being so delusional that she thought she might be that woman. She was aware of a tingle at the end of her nose a second before she felt the well of wetness in her eyes. With panic rising, she knew she needed to escape her own self-centred behaviour and focus on Alison. After all, that was what she was being paid to do and she had a duty of care.

Olivia took a tissue from the side, blew her nose, and cleared her throat.

"Sorry. Hay fever," Olivia mumbled, pulling down the sleeve of her blouse where it had wrinkled.

"At the end of November?" The amused twinkle in her eyes softened Alison's sceptical tone.

"Have you spoken to Victoria and Abby about this?" Olivia was determined to forge ahead to regain her professional composure.

Alison shook her head. "Not in so many words. Things have changed, our relationship has changed. Rather than being a mistress with two subs, we're three strong women enjoying each other's company, all of whom love each other. But I think Victoria knows even that has a time limit. She said herself it's all part of the healing process, and I'd be the first to agree it's a process. I feel I'm coming to the end of this part of the process."

Olivia's pen stilled, and she glanced up from her pad. "What do you mean?"

"I need to talk to them. I need to be honest about what I feel. And I couldn't have gotten to this point, in being able to own all of *this*, without you."

Olivia could feel her heart thump in her chest, blood rushing through her ears.

"That's the other thing that needs to change. I've come such a long way thanks to the work we've done and I'll always be really grateful—" Alison leant forward in her chair and for a moment Olivia thought she was about to reach out for her hand but she didn't, instead she just stared straight into her eyes and said, "To get what I really want I need to leave therapy. I want this to be my last session."

Olivia's jaw dropped, and the swell of emotion she'd been so desperately trying to swallow down was rapidly rising to the surface again. She couldn't—no, she wouldn't—allow herself to lose control. If she did, it would only prove Alison's decision to cease therapy to be the correct way forward.

"D-don't you think that's a bit soon? I-I mean to just…it's very abrupt. Normally what I would do is reduce the frequency of the sessions, not end them immediately. We might move to every other week?"

Alison laughed. "Isn't it supposed to be the client who gets angsty about finishing these things?" Her grin was wicked.

But Olivia looked at her seriously. "Alison, I think we need to talk about this. This isn't some flippant decision that you can just make."

"Olivia, you won't change my mind. I need to end this to—"

There was no way Olivia could allow her to keep talking. She needed to take charge, if only to stop herself from having an emotional breakdown in front of the woman.

"It's Dr Hopkins, as I've reminded you several times now. If you've decided, there is little I can do. If you can speak to Sharon on the way out, cancel any future appointments you've scheduled previously and settle any outstanding invoices, please." Olivia stood, walking rapidly to her desk and the safety of shuffling papers. Tears brimmed in her eyes, desperate to free themselves from the temporary suspension in which they were held. *Just hold on. Just hold on,* Olivia repeated to herself as a huge sob tried to lodge itself in her throat.

"But Olivia I want to—"

"The session is over, Alison. Please see yourself out."

Olivia didn't dare turn around as she heard Alison prepare to leave. If she were to look into the face of the woman she had spent so much time yearning for, then she would surely break into a thousand pieces. The soft sound of the door closing let Olivia know she was alone. With her hands braced against the hard edge of her desk, the sob she had battled so hard to suppress broke free, releasing a cascade of never-ending tears. What a fool she had been to have dreamt the impossible.

Chapter 24
DR OLIVIA HOPKINS

Olivia turned her coffee cup around in its saucer nervously, then picked up the empty sugar packet, before folding it one way, then the other. Right now, she'd do almost anything to distract herself from thinking about the conversation she was about to have.

This was her first visit back to Greens of George Street since that fateful morning where she'd sat at the window table, waiting for Victoria to emerge from the office building opposite. But today she hadn't chosen a window table, instead she'd opted for a booth in the darkest corner of the establishment. The admissions she was about to make may cleanse her soul, but she didn't want anyone else to hear as she threw herself at the mercy of Victoria Fraser.

Perched on the little black leather banquette, Olivia kept glancing towards the front of the cafe, cursing herself for arranging this meeting. Years ago, with the entry of every new patron, a small brass bell would sound, struck by the movement of the door, but the recent modernisation meant Olivia wouldn't benefit from the antique early warning system.

No matter how nerve wracking this was for Olivia—and it was—Victoria deserved honesty, as well as a full and frank explanation for her bizarre behaviour. The last number of days since Alison had walked out of her office and her life, had left Olivia with endless hours of soul searching, as well as enormous pain. A pain like she had never experienced before. It cut to the very core of her being, leaving her bereft, floundering and lost. She'd been a fool, a stupid schoolgirl with an uncontrollable crush, but worse than any of that, she'd been unethical having overstepped the professional boundaries by such a large margin she could no longer see safety. Olivia was an incompetent therapist and an awful human being…that had been her most recent mantra. Lost in self-flagellation, she hadn't been aware of Victoria's arrival until she was halfway up the long, thin cafe. The woman never failed to take her breath away.

Unbuttoning her longline military jacket with one hand, Victoria glanced from side to side, obviously looking for where Olivia was sitting. Olivia did a slight wave of the hand, as if she was a five-year-old in class. The only thing she was missing was a *Please, Miss. It must look pathetic.*

It certainly felt pathetic. But then, hadn't her entire behaviour up to this point been pathetic? Internally, she cringed. *Oh god, why did I arrange this?*

Victoria approached the table, shrugging herself out of her jacket, and Olivia stood, thankful for the constraints of the booth, otherwise she might have been overcome with a compulsion to curtsy or, at the very least, bow.

Victoria nodded and then frowned, waving her hand. "Sit."

Olivia did as she was told.

"Dr Olivia Hopkins. I'm delighted to meet you," Victoria said with a tight smile, offering her hand as though this was the first time the two women had met.

"Um, yes. But you can call me Olivia," Olivia offered with a shy blush.

"Are you sure you don't want me to call you Kerry?" Victoria's eyes glimmered with humour.

Olivia realised one of them was enjoying this encounter far more than the other. "No, Olivia is fine. I suppose I should start with an apology." Olivia's blush deepened as she confronted the very real mortification resulting from her behaviour.

Thankfully, she was saved by the waiter who stood with his pen against his pad, ready to take the order. "Good morning," he said brightly.

"Morning," said Victoria. "I'll have, umm…" She looked at the menu. "A pot of green tea, please, and Olivia, what would you like?"

Olivia glanced down at her cup; it was nearly finished. "Just a flat white, please," she said, looking up at the waiter almost apologetically. Olivia pondered on how her order reflected her mood, as the waiter recorded their selection with a quick flick of the stylus on the electronic pad and hastily disappeared.

"So," said Victoria. "Do you want to explain why we're here?"

Olivia inhaled a deep breath, steadying herself. As much as she had tried to rehearse this moment, having run through what she wanted to say in her head multiple times, all the scripted lines eluded her. How could she possibly explain what she'd done?

Stumbling about in her head wasn't producing anything coherent, so she fell back on her many years of psychotherapy training. Deflect and ask a question.

"Can I ask, how did you know who I was? And," she paused, because this was the burning, shameful question she had to know the answer to. "How long have you known I wasn't who I claimed to be?"

Victoria leant forward, placing an elbow on the table and rested her chin on her hand, then met Olivia's gaze. "Let me see. I think that would have been right after the first phone call we had."

Olivia's eyes widened in surprise. "You mean you knew before you met me?"

Victoria nodded. "I suspected," she said. "But it wasn't until I came and met you I knew for sure. If you're going to assume somebody else's identity, especially that of your…is it your sister?" Victoria asked, raising her eyebrows in question. Olivia nodded dumbly. "Then you should make sure that she doesn't have a photo on her LinkedIn profile."

"Oh," was all that Olivia could say, having decided that a career in espionage was perhaps out of her reach.

"When I walked up the stairs and saw you, I knew immediately that you weren't Kerry Patterson and that my gut had been correct. From there it was a simple search of the address where we met, the flat, via the land registry, and that told me it was co-owned by a Dr Olivia Hopkins, and Lucas Lawson, who I believe is your ex-husband?"

Olivia once again nodded dumbly. God, she had underestimated Victoria, and well and truly overestimated her powers of deceit. Lucas had always claimed that he could tell when she was lying, and for Olivia that should have been enough of a forewarning, given she'd always considered Lucas borderline.

"But none of that is important," Victoria said. "I'm interested in why you went to such lengths. It's my turn to play the therapist and I'm interested in your motivations."

Olivia winced as Victoria said the word *play*. It was a pointed reminder of her unforgivable behaviour in playing with a client's mental health. If Victoria didn't expose her,

Olivia knew she would have to report herself as misconduct of this magnitude couldn't be allowed to go unaddressed. But that was for tomorrow, today she needed to find the answers she owed Victoria.

"I-I," Olivia faltered. "I wanted to understand Alison and her situation better. I've not had a client in a polyamorous relationship before and given Alison's previous trauma, I wanted to make sure I offered her appropriate support."

"Really? Are we going to do this? You're going to hide behind a lie of support?" Victoria's tone did nothing to hide her incredulity. "Or can we cut to the chase and have some honesty?" There was no hint of humour in either Victoria's tone or expression. "I've got a busy day and I don't have time to sit and listen to untruths. You have a choice, Olivia, because everything in life is about choice. Start being honest or I'll just take my green tea to go."

The waiter appeared with their drinks, and Olivia was thankful for the few seconds of reprieve his appearance offered, but all too soon he'd gone again, leaving Olivia no place to hide. She swallowed. None of the explanations which she had rehearsed were going to cut the mustard today. "I can't defend my actions. They were—I was ethically and morally wrong on every level."

Olivia glanced up, trying to gauge Victoria's response to her candour, but the woman was giving nothing away.

"Something happened with Alison, something that's never happened with any other client. I've a reputation as being a stickler for boundaries, but—" Olivia shook her head. "I couldn't stop thinking about her. At first I put it down to wanting to ensure I was offering her the best therapy because she'd pop into my head when I was making dinner or coming to work on the bus…but the more I saw her, the more she was all I could think about. I'd wake up in the morning and be lying in bed, wondering what it'd be like to have her lying next to me, or I'd be watching a movie, wondering if she'd seen it. I don't even know what her favourite movie is."

Olivia let out a huff of air, but Victoria's expression was inscrutable. It didn't matter, she was in free flow with honesty and there was little point in stopping now. If Victoria was going to take her to task, then Olivia had just handed her all the required ammunition. She might as well unburden herself and help squeeze the trigger.

"I couldn't stop thinking about her, and this might sound ridiculous now, but I thought if you could teach me then maybe she might start thinking of me as more than just her therapist, like someone who had something to offer her." Olivia felt the warmth of tears coat her eyes. "I'm sorry... about everything. I got everything so spectacularly wrong and now she's walked away from her therapy."

Victoria narrowed her eyes, considering the woman. "Is this concern about Alison or concern about yourself?" Victoria asked in a flat, measured tone.

Olivia thought for a moment. She wanted to say it was over concern for Alison because that's what any good therapist would say, but she knew it wasn't strictly true. On reflection with any other therapist, Alison would have been nearing a natural conclusion to her sessions, but because Olivia hadn't wanted to lose contact, she may have drawn out the therapeutic relationship for longer than required. Just another way she'd broken the ethics by which she was professionally bound.

"It's out of concern for myself," Olivia admitted, staring down at her untouched flat white. A thin skin had formed over the cold, murky-looking liquid. Knowing honesty was the only path available, she forged on. "They always warn you when dealing with clients that there's a certain element of transference, and people always think that it's the client rather than the therapist, but this was all me. I couldn't stop thinking about her and in some small way, I'd convinced myself I loved her." Olivia watched as Victoria cocked her head as though she might speak. "I know it isn't right and I should have recused myself, but...I couldn't. All I can think about is Alison and in some twisted way I thought if you could teach me how to be you, then there might be space for me in her life."

Victoria sat and stared. If she had been about to speak, she'd changed her mind. Olivia wasn't sure what to make of it. She thought she might have gotten angry, but Victoria wasn't angry. She looked almost disappointed.

"Olivia, in the time that I started training you, what was it about the four pillars you didn't understand? Respect, honesty, choice, and consent. Without these four pillars, everything falls apart—as you found out."

Olivia blushed. Victoria was right, and it had been a painful lesson to learn.

"If you respect someone, then you'll offer them honesty and allow them to choose what's right for them and from there they will either give you consent, or not, and as we both know, consent is vital. It represents a human's ethical and legal right for self-determination."

Olivia knew that Victoria's choice of words around the ethical framework hadn't been plucked out of the air, nor was she referring solely to lifestyle choices because it was part and parcel of the Hippocratic oath she swore to uphold. Olivia shrank from her usual 5'5" down to just 5" but Victoria didn't slow down.

"You can't force someone to be with you. They have to be with you because they want to be, and they can only make that choice if they know exactly who you are. That takes honesty and respect, both qualities that I know Alison would have shown you in abundance. I know Alison, and I know how vulnerable she would have been."

The sting of tears burnt Olivia's eyes. She had made so many mistakes, been so selfish, and here she was, confessing to a woman who had obviously decided her career was not worth saving. Right now, Olivia agreed. For all the years that she had fought to forge her reputation, none of it seemed important anymore, not in the face of losing Alison.

"I'm sorry," she mumbled, shame seeping through every part of her body. "I betrayed her trust and all because I was so infatuated I thought I could be her new domme."

Victoria laughed. "You think Alison needs a new domme?" Then she smiled a broad, warm smile and Olivia found herself both flustered and confused.

"I know she wants…she wants—" Olivia stopped herself. She was about to breach her code of ethics again, not that it would have made any difference now. The actions she'd already taken would have her struck off. But she couldn't bring herself to say what Alison had told her. Respect. She had to give Alison respect.

Victoria laughed. "Let me guess, she wants more intensity. She is looking for *someone*, rather than two people." She raised her eyebrows in question and Olivia glanced away. Victoria had guessed, but then again, Victoria had probably known all the way along.

"Dr Olivia Hopkins, I happen to think you are a very good therapist. Alison has benefitted from seeing you, although your methods are more than a little unorthodox. You are not a bad person." Victoria leaned forward and put her hand over hers. "You helped Alison find herself again and for that, we're all very grateful."

There was a *but* coming, Olivia could feel it.

"But—I also think you're a hopeless case. You'll never be a dominatrix. It's not in your character and if you stop and take a cold, hard look at what sits between you and Alison, then you might see she would never have wanted you in that way." Victoria's voice was warm but it didn't stop her words cutting like a knife through Olivia's heart. This was the level of honesty she should have encompassed.

"I know she doesn't want me. That's abundantly clear." For all of Olivia's guilt, she still couldn't stop the edge of hurt in her voice. "And I know I'm not a domme by any stretch of the imagination. My reactions to your…directions showed me that much." Removing her hand from Victoria's, she brought it up to wipe away her tears. "When you…oh, I can't even say it out loud. I-I've never been so turned on."

This wasn't the type of conversation the usual patrons of Greens of George Street were used to, and with an average age of seventy-two, Olivia would usually have refrained from such conversations over coffee, but today she didn't care whether or not they heard her.

Victoria slid her hand across the table, seeing Olivia's obvious discomfort and taking her hand again, she squeezed it. "I know you enjoyed being submissive. You got a thrill from it. I could hear it down the line. All I'm going to say to you is, don't lose heart." Again, she gave a warm smile. "Look, we're having a party in December. Why don't you come? Come as my guest. It's over in Aberdour."

Olivia screwed her face up in confusion. Victoria should end her career, not invite her to a party.

"It's a masquerade ball. I'll send you an outfit to wear. All I ask is that you trust me and I'll look after you. And you never know, you might get more than you bargained for."

"I can't be your sub, I—" Olivia's panic trembled through her voice, but Victoria just laughed.

"You're not my sub, and I'm certainly not your mistress. I want you to trust me. But…" Victoria gave a playful shrug. "It's your choice to come. It's always your choice to come."

Chapter 25
ALISON

It had been several days since Alison's final encounter with Olivia and her abrupt ejection from the woman's office. Since that moment, the thought of which still made her wince, she'd been licking her wounds. Having Abby declare her as prematurely peri-menopausal because she was so moody hadn't helped, so she'd hidden herself away from the world in the sanctuary of her studio during the day. Even at night, she could no longer take solace from the comfort of being with Victoria and Abby. It had all just become so over-whelming she'd feigned headaches for the last two nights, retiring early to be on her own.

The strategy was to say thanks and goodbye to Dr Olivia Hopkins, the therapist, and hello to Olivia, the stunning woman who had been filling her daydreams for way too long. Alison had even made them dinner reservations at Gosier after Victoria had raved about its wine list, she was so sure Olivia would agree. Thank god she hadn't asked for the 96 Chateau d'Yquem Sauternes to be put on ice.

Even looking back on it now, Alison wasn't sure where her meticulous planning had let her down. Right up to when she was ordered to show herself out, Alison had thought that the two of them were on the same page. Adding insult to injury had been Sharon, receptionist extraordinaire, who seemed to take delight in Alison's confusion and distress. How the hell a woman like that had secured a position dealing with vulnerable people beggared belief. Not that Alison considered herself to be vulnerable. Olivia had helped her with that.

Throughout their sessions, Alison had given everything she had on the understanding that talking would help. With the exception of Victoria, Olivia knew more about her than anyone else in her whole wide world, which—thanks to Mhairi and her after effects—really wasn't that large. With Olivia gone and having consciously distanced herself from Victoria and Abby, physically and perhaps emotionally, Alison felt terrifyingly alone, and all of it was of her own doing. The ache in her chest made her question if she'd been making wise choices, especially regarding her therapy sessions.

"Penny for them?" Victoria asked, laying a hand on Alison's forearm.

Alison wondered if she should tell them what she'd uncovered in her quest for self-discovery, but with Abby standing on the high platform of Callie's new tailor shop, being pinned into an exquisite deep red satin sub outfit, and chatting at speed about the Christmas party, she wasn't sure if now was the time. Ironically, after months of spilling her guts on everything she'd repressed for years, Alison had spent the last few days guarding her emotions from the outside world as though they were a precious manuscript she was shielding from the rain.

"I've something to tell you," Alison blurted. "Both of you."

Abby didn't appear to hear her and kept talking. "Bryce is

coming, and he's sending some surprises up beforehand, but he won't tell us what they are."

But Victoria had heard her, and she glanced in Alison's direction, narrowing her eyes. Waving one hand towards Abby, she said, "Abby, darling, I think Alison wants to tell us something."

Alison had this uncanny notion that Victoria knew what she was about to say, but it didn't make it any easier. "I—okay," she sighed. "I've been making a few changes, and not just my hair." She gave a nervous chuckle at her own humour, running her hands through the soft fuzz at the side. "I've, um, completed my therapy."

Victoria nodded. Abby just stood looking at her. Callie didn't look up but kept pinning.

"I've come a long way since…Mhairi—and the therapy has allowed me to work through my issues, helping me figure out what I want." Alison took a deep breath, knowing she had to finish what she'd started. "Things between us have changed and I want to explore different things…extracurricular things."

Abby squealed as Callie stuck a pin in her thigh. "Ow!"

"Oh, sorry," said Callie, looking like she was trying desperately to melt into the flowery wallpaper.

"What do you mean, you want to explore different things?" Abby asked, rubbing the soft skin on the inside of her thigh where the pin had entered.

"Sorry," mumbled Callie.

"I might want to have encounters with more than just the two of you." Alison tried to explain as discreetly as she could, given they were in company. With hindsight perched on her shoulder, she realised this had been entirely the wrong time for this discussion.

Abby screwed her face up. "What are you talking about?"

She let out a long exasperated sigh, and looked pleadingly

at Victoria for help, but Victoria said nothing. This, Alison realised, had to come from her and her alone. "I'd like to see other people."

"You're leaving us?" Abby's voice raised as quickly as her eyebrows.

"Well, I'm not leaving you. I just…" Alison desperately tried to find the words. She felt a terrible guilt crush down upon her. "I just want…oh god. Look, I love you both and I… I know you love me, but it's different for the two of you. You've got each other and I'm the third cog. We don't love each other in the same way. Abby, if you had to choose between me and Victoria, Victoria would win every time."

"Well, yeah," said Abby incredulously. "She's my mistress, but she's your mistress too."

Alison tried not to roll her eyes. This was going to be harder than she thought. "If Victoria had to choose." She put her hand up in defence. "And I'm not saying Victoria would have to choose, but if Victoria had to choose, she would choose you, because the bond that the two of you share is stronger than the bond that I have with either of you."

Abby still didn't look like she was understanding what was being said. "We aren't enough for you?" she asked.

Alison grimaced. This was achingly similar to the painful conversation she'd had with Victoria all those years before. "I'm not saying that. Well, I sort of am saying that. As much as I love you," Alison's tone became gentler, "sometimes love isn't enough, Abby."

Abby looked like she was about to burst into tears. It was only when Victoria saw her bottom lip quiver did she intervene. Standing, she made her way across to Abby. "Callie, could you give us just a moment, please?" Callie, with a mouth full of pins, nodded, looking relieved at being allowed to escape. Alison wanted to join her.

Victoria placed a hand on either side of Abby's shoulders.

"Look, this is what we discussed before. Alison is finding herself again. She's exploring different things, and sometimes she will need to explore things without us. But no matter what happens, you are always enough. Do you hear me?"

Abby pulled her lips together to form a tight line. She looked like a five-year-old that had just been told she couldn't go to the safari park. Victoria then turned her attention to Alison.

"I understand. I hear you and I see you. You know there's always a place here for you, with us. And I think it's fairly obvious that Abby has a very large soft spot for you. She loves you, and I do, too. But I hear what you're saying and, yes, you're right. If I had to choose, I would choose Abby, so I can't deny you that same connection with someone else."

Alison breathed out an enormous sigh of relief. She should have known to trust Victoria. In all the years they had known and loved each other, she'd never let her down.

"Have you met somebody?" Victoria asked.

"I met someone I was interested in, but it wasn't mutual, so no." Alison shook her head.

"Come here," said Victoria, beckoning Alison forward. She pushed herself up from the chair and took the three steps across to where Victoria and Abby stood. "We love you very much and nothing will change that. And you're still welcome with us, every night and every day, until you find your person."

"Thank you," said Alison. "I was frightened you wouldn't understand or think me ungrateful."

"Oh, I understand. I think everybody should be lucky enough to find their Abby." Victoria smiled, looking up at the younger woman who was standing on the platform. Placing one hand behind Abby's neck, Victoria pulled her down into a kiss, and then whispered in her ear, "Alison deserves to find somebody as amazing as you."

Abby just nodded.

"And you," Victoria said, placing her hands on Alison's shoulders and leaning in until their foreheads touched, "you deserve the very best. We're all adults here and we all love each other, that's all that matters. We'll find a way through as long as we're honest with each other." Placing her lips against Alison's, Victoria kissed her passionately and Alison responded in kind.

It was only when their lips parted Victoria whispered, "I'll always love you." Then she looked up at Abby. "And Abby, the devotion that you give me is the devotion that somebody should give to Alison."

Abby didn't seem to understand. "But Alison's a sub. Shouldn't she be devoted to somebody else? Is she... Alison, do you want a new mistress?"

Alison's face flushed, and she gave a slight shake of her head. "I-I...I don't think so," she stammered. This time, much to Alison's relief, Victoria came to her rescue.

"Abby, just like sexuality, it's a spectrum. Different people bring out different parts of our personalities, and the dynamics of every arrangement vary. The way Alison is, or had been with us, doesn't dictate the way any new relationship might play out. No two combinations are ever the same, because we are all unique. Wonderfully, gloriously unique. Never make assumptions based on what's gone before, because people can surprise the hell out of you."

Abby nodded, offering an apologetic lopsided grin to Alison, who was now feeling a little bad for her young lover, who'd been stuck with pins because of her timing. But then, lots of people liked a little belonephilia, and she was still exploring so...

"And as for you," Victoria turned back to Alison, who looked up to see her ex-mistress smiling, "I hope you never stop surprising me because I am so very proud of you."

Chapter 26
VICTORIA

The thirty-foot-high Christmas tree, adorned with gold and white decorations and emblazoned with more than a thousand fairy lights, sat in pride of place in the enormous window of the Aberdour property. Even the large St Andrew's Cross, which dominated the centre of the open plan room, had a little Santa hat on the top corner and tinsel to make it look slightly less imposing. The party was a full day away, so in theory there was no rush, but Victoria looked at the vast pile of tinsel at Abby's feet and sighed. It was going to be a long day.

Just as she was about to comment on the fact they had more decorations (and toys) than Hamley's, her phone burst into life displaying Gareth's name, and with perfect synchronisation, the doorbell rang.

"I'll get it!" Abby jumped down from the steps she'd been using to pop the naked Santa bauble on the tree (one of the most popular from their new *Christmas pornament* range) and ran towards the door, leaving a bemused Alison still clutching the ladder. Victoria shook her head, tapped the iPhone screen and brought it to her ear.

"Hi, Victoria." Gareth's immediate greeting surprised her. She hadn't even said hello.

"Gareth, is everything all right?" Victoria could hear the tension in his greeting, and it alarmed her.

"Yes," he said. "Everything is fine. In fact, I'm calling with good news."

"Good news?" Victoria stared intently out the window over the frost-topped fields. It was mid-afternoon, but as the sun broke through the white bulge of cumulus clouds, the temperature was only just rising above freezing. Watching the steam rise from the thawing dark soil, Victoria knew what she wanted Gareth to say. It was the only news she'd consider being good.

"We think we've found Mhairi, or at least we think we know where she is. A farmhouse, not far from Galashiels in the Borders. The place is pretty remote, about three miles from the main road. It would appear that one of her previous colleagues has given her refuge. Tip-off came from a farm-hand. We're watching the place just now for confirmation and depending on what we see, we'll raid the property, tomorrow night at the latest."

"At night?" Victoria asked. "Don't you normally do raids first thing in the morning?"

"Have you been watching crime dramas again, Detective Fraser?" Gareth laughed. "Yeah, we do, but we'll have eyes on the house. If she is there, she won't be able to leave without us knowing. The property is so remote that if we try to approach during the day, they'll see us coming and there's a good chance she'll run. Darkness is our friend."

Victoria nodded, more to herself than anybody else. It seemed sensible. They were only five days away from the shortest day of the year and even now, by about 3 p.m., twilight was emerging.

"Okay," she said. "I can't tell you how relieved I am that you've got her."

"We don't yet, but we will in a matter of hours. There's no way she'll get bail and we've an extradition treaty with Thailand, so she's fucked. They'll make an example of her." Gareth gave what Victoria could only describe as an evil *snort*.

"Okay, will you call me when you've got her? We've got the party tomorrow night. It's a shame that you and Lauren couldn't make it. Pass on my love to her, will you?"

"Yeah, of course," he said. "Have a good party."

Victoria inhaled deeply. As much as she'd liked to have Gareth and Lauren join them for the festivities, and not just because he was a sight to behold in a gimp outfit, having Gareth wipe Mhairi from their lives was far more valuable. She'd recompense him in due course. Tomorrow would reset many boundaries, but none more so than the exclusion of Mhairi from their lives, for good.

"What have you ordered?" Alison's voice brought Victoria back into the room and she turned to see both women hauling a huge box covered with UPS stickers.

"I don't know. What is it?" Victoria asked, and then she remembered the conversation she'd had with Bryce last week. "Open nothing unless there are explicit instructions giving you permission."

Both Alison and Abby stared at her as though she'd lost her mind.

"Bryce said he was sending some toys. There's one you're allowed to open because he's asked us to set it up, and before you ask, no, I don't know what's in them."

Victoria glanced at her watch. It was 3:20 p.m. Callie was due at half past and there was still bloody tinsel everywhere.

"Christ, these are heavy." Alison moaned, clutching her back as they finished hauling the second of the enormous boxes.

Victoria wandered over and looked at the outsized cardboard boxes. The first was at least five feet long by three feet wide. Not unsubstantial, the second was shorter but much wider. That was the package that seemed to break Alison's back. Victoria was surprised that Bryce hadn't been forced to deliver them by pallet. The third and last box was much smaller and, thankfully, lighter. But it was the first box that had a large label on the front in bold black lettering, 'Set Me Up'.

How very Bryce, Victoria thought.

"So we only open this one?" Abby pointed the loosely gripped scissors towards the largest box. Victoria nodded, turning her attention back to tidying tinsel as she heard the thick tape being sliced open.

"OMG! I haven't seen one of these in years, not since Mhairi..." Alison's voice trailed off as though lost in thought.

Victoria turned back, looking towards the box. "What is it?"

Abby twisted her head from one side to the other. "I've no idea, but it reminds me of this play tent I had as a kid."

"This is a completely different kind of play tent," Alison said with a wicked grin. "It's a latex vacuum bed."

"Oh, christ." Victoria rolled her eyes. *Trust Bryce.* Abby handed her the envelope, which contained a note from Bryce.

Hi Vicks, it started. Victoria hated when Bryce called her Vicks. That was a menthol inhalant, but she continued to read out loud so that Abby and Alison could hear. "Hi Vicks," she said, rolling her eyes. "Thought this might be useful for tomorrow. Really looking forward to seeing you. Please have a play ahead of time. Love, Bryce."

"I still don't know what it is." Abby held two long lengths of plastic poles that formed the frame.

"We'll build it and then you'll see." Alison took the poles from Abby's hands. "Help me get the rest of this out."

Between the three of them, they carefully emptied the contents of the box. *If Ikea got kinky,* Victoria mused as she laid out the framework. Rolling out the *tent,* as Abby called it, they placed the partially connected framework in place and then, in situ, snapped in the last couple of poles which made the latex covering taut.

"It's like a massive plastic envelope." Abby stared at it, unable to hide her horror. "Surely you don't get inside that, do you?"

Both Victoria and Alison gave a solemn nod, then Alison held open the edge.

"Not a fucking chance!"

"No? You're not willing to slide in while I suck the air out?" Alison asked, brandishing the long tube which was attached to the mini vacuum, waving it in the air.

"How the hell do you breathe?"

"The breathing hole is here." Alison stuck her fingers into the tiny oval hole. "You slide in through the edge and then it gets zipped up. This," Alison waved the tube again, "goes in here and then we switch it on and the air gets sucked out. You can't move. If someone wants to be very cruel, they'll strap a vibrator to you before they start the vacuum."

Abby's face paled, and Alison bent over, laughing. "I'm going to go out on a limb here and guess this maybe isn't your jam?"

"The only thing I thought you vacuumed in bags was left-over food, not people."

"Well, that explains the dust in your studio," Victoria teased.

"How can anybody think that's sexy?" she asked.

Both Alison and Victoria looked at each other and shrugged. "We won't be trying it out, but Bryce seems very keen. Help me move it to the back room. I'm not sure everyone will appreciate it, so perhaps it's best out of the main area. We'll move the other boxes in there too, and he can decide what he wants to do with them."

They were just laying it against the wall when the doorbell rang and the door almost immediately opened.

"Hellooo, it's me." Callie's voice sounded through the house. This had been her first time here. She walked in, looked at the St Andrew's Cross and gasped, "Oh, my."

Victoria gave her a hug. "Thanks so much for coming out, Callie."

"Oh, no worries. I was intrigued to see the place before tomorrow night." Glancing over at the set of stocks, one of Alison's latest projects, she raised her eyebrows. "For me, this is going to be quite the experience."

"Hopefully, but one you will enjoy from a business perspective. Everyone here will be a potential new client," Victoria assured her.

"Mm." Callie pulled the garment carriers from her arm, holding up the first one. "This one's yours," she said to Abby, "and this is yours." Callie handed an identical long black nylon carrier to Victoria. "And this one, my darling, is yours." Callie gave Alison both the carrier and a quick wink, much to Victoria's surprise. Perhaps Callie would enjoy the party more than she had expected.

"Now all of you," Callie said, clapping her hands. "Go try them on, then I can do any final nips and tucks."

Victoria and Abby immediately stripped down, ready to try on Callie's creations, but Alison nodded to the bathroom. "I'm just going to nip in here and get changed."

Abby flashed Victoria a quizzical glance.

"I want to see myself in it first," Alison said, and Victoria immediately knew why. There was no secret to either Victoria's or Abby's choice for the party because they had tried them on when they'd been together, but not Alison. She had chosen to have a private fitting, waiting until they had left. Alison had mentioned nothing specifically, but Victoria suspected it might not be her usual style.

"Come on, slowcoach," said Victoria to Abby, turning her attention away from Alison and back to both her and Abby's state of undress.

Abby had chosen something that wouldn't look out of place in Santa's grotto. *Albeit a damned sexy grotto*, thought Victoria. It was cute, in red and green with white edging, and had straps with tiny slits which crossed over her breasts; manipulated in the right way, the slits would allow her nipples, when erect, to pop through. Again, she wore her favourite type of satin briefs, the ones with studs that, when pulled apart, made the whole thing crotchless.

Victoria had chosen an outfit of black and red, a startling number of silk and lace, that hugged her figure and pushed her breasts high and together. Pulling herself to her full height, she then bent over as though she were trying to touch her toes.

"That works for me," Abby said with a cheeky grin.

"Alterations?" Callie asked, but they both shook their heads.

"They're perfect, as always." Victoria smoothed her hands over the bones of the bodice, enjoying the mixture of smooth and rough the materials offered.

"Holy shit, Alison, that's so fucking hot!"

Victoria turned, curious to see what had caused Abby's outburst, and she, too, had eyebrows that shot into her hair-line as she took in a transformed Alison. Rather than the usual sub outfit of a leather harness, Alison wore tight leather chaps and a stiff black leather Bavarian under-bust corset which pushed her ample breast up and out. The entire look was finished with the now short blonde hair.

Victoria whistled, and Abby, suddenly finding the power of speech again, blurted, "It's just as well you weren't wearing that when we tested out your swing thing."

Alison laughed nervously, aware that her ex-mistress was giving Abby a long, hard stare.

"What did you just say, my Pet?"

"I just...there's, uh..." stammered Abby. "Sorry, Mistress."

"I should think so, too," said Victoria, not hiding her smile. "So all we need now are the masks."

Callie opened the large round box to her side and handed each of them the pièce de résistance.

"At least it means I won't have to watch you drool over Alison." Victoria placed the leather mask over her cheeks and weaved the tie through her red hair, securing it tightly at the back of her head.

Alison and Abby did the same, marvelling at how unlike themselves they now looked.

Chapter 27

ABBY

Abby slipped her arm through Victoria's and listened to her mistress sweet-talk clients and friends alike. Jenny came over, clutching what looked like a scotch over ice. Abby looked around but Darian, her *lodger,* wasn't in tow.

"On your own?" Victoria asked.

"Uh-huh. Darian has moved back to Newcastle. She's got family down there." Jenny swigged a generous mouthful from her glass. "I encouraged her to make contact. She was reluctant at first but it seems she and her nan had more in common than they thought: an endless amount of hatred for her mother."

"On the lookout for a new sub?" Victoria asked playfully, and Jenny choked on her drink.

"Darian was never mine, way too young. I'm more likely to be interested in her nan. But a new sub might be a welcome distraction. Got a Christmas present lined up for me anywhere?" Jenny turned, surveying the room with a devilish smile.

Abby was a little surprised that Jenny and Darian had never become an item. Sure, there was a sizable age gap of thirtyish years, she reckoned, but still… Darian doted on Jenny. Wherever Jenny went, Darian had to follow.

"There are a few fresh faces here tonight, so you never know." Victoria laid a hand over Abby's, stroking it slowly.

"I can see you won't be letting this one go anytime soon," Jenny chuckled.

Abby smiled demurely, playing the devoted sub to the end.

"Abby has stolen my heart. Haven't you, my Pet?" Victoria ran her fingertips up the length of Abby's arm, causing her to shiver in excitement. "But Jenny, if I come across a mature and willing sub, I'll point them in your direction. You'll have to forgive us. We need to do the rounds, I'm afraid, and say hello to everyone before we can really enjoy ourselves."

Abby felt Victoria's fingertips caress the side of her breasts, and she inhaled sharply. Her mistress was obviously feeling frisky tonight, and that thought brought with it another twitch of arousal. She would have been happy for Victoria to continue the fingertip search of her body, but then a sight from the other side of the room stopped her dead in her tracks.

"Mistress, Matt has arrived. May I…"

Abby dropped a light kiss on Victoria's cheek, and, turning to welcome Matt, she stifled a giggle.

"What the hell are you wearing?" Abby reached down to touch the mound of nylon-esque furball sprouting from his crotch. A shock of static shot through her arm and she pulled back sharply just as Matt jolted his arse back, obviously experiencing the same shock, but in a much more sensitive way. "You could have warned me it bites," she said, rubbing her shocked finger.

"I'd like to say the bark is much worse than its bite, but trust me, it's not. Ooh—" Matt's eyes rolled back, and grunting, he arched his back as though he was about to break into a medical seizure or… *Please god no*, thought Abby, *please don't orgasm in front of me.* But just as quickly as his little episode started, it stopped. Standing naked apart from a pair of rainbow Crocs (not his best look) and what looked to be a dead ferret munching on his unmentionables, he offered a sleepy grin.

"Matt, what the—really?"

"I'm back with Nylon Norman," he whispered theatrically, and through heavy lids, he glanced over to a chap in a sheer nylon body suit. Abby had no idea they came in that width, nor that denier. One thing that was for sure was that he'd be laddered to buggery by the end of the night.

"The furry rabbit thing," Matt motioned to his groin, "helps conduct the static charge, and Norman, the rascal, has me wearing an electrically charged butt plug, so you could say I'm a little wired."

Abby stared at him. "And the footwear?"

"I've sixty volts flooding through my body when he hits his little red button, so I thought for everyone's sake it was probably better I ground myself."

"Matt, you're the least grounded person I know."

"Here," Matt held his hands out to Abby, "take my hands and I'll share some of my juice with you."

Abby jumped back about six feet. "I'm not touching anything, live or dead." Her eyes dropped to the ball of fur. "If that thing so much as moves…"

"Abby, my Pet…" Victoria's appearance brought a rush of relief, as well as a welcome escape to Abby, who could swear the ferret was twitching. "Matt, I'm so glad you made it."

Abby watched as her mistress took in Matt's naked torso and then sunk lower. One eyebrow arched, and her hand fluttered over her chest, not in excitement, rather in a way that suggested Victoria's gag reflex might kick in. But that might have been the sight of the Crocs.

"Abby, I'm sorry to interrupt you, but I wanted to introduce you to Olivia. You remember Olivia, don't you?"

"You mean…" Abby looked at her mistress, eyes widening. Victoria simply nodded.

The woman at Victoria's side was dressed in a similar way to Abby, but instead of red satin, hers was ivory and adorned with bright yellow daisies. There was something pornographically innocent about the combination in a sub's attire.

"Hi, Olivia." Abby smiled, taking in the woman's body. Although she couldn't see her face under the white leather mask, adorned with what looked like plumage, the delicate pitting of cellulite over her thighs and the beginning of a cute apron suggested Olivia to be of a similar age to Victoria, just less well-preserved. Not that she had a vast experience with older women. Victoria was her only foray into women in their forties, and Victoria was anything but typical.

"I was wondering if you could introduce Olivia to Alison, my Pet. I'd do it myself, but I need to call Gareth. I've had several missed calls. He might want to give me some good news. You don't mind, do you?"

Abby assured Victoria she'd be happy to make the introductions and then leant forward, whispering loudly into Olivia's ear, "Have you put your balls in?"

The plume of scarlet started at the low cut of Olivia's bra and rose rapidly until even the scalp under her strawberry blonde waves seemed to colour.

Victoria laughed.

"I'm only teasing." Abby squeezed Olivia's hand.

"Abby, behave yourself and try to keep Olivia out of Jenny's sight. If she sees her, she'll be hornier than a rhino." Victoria gave a light kiss to Olivia's cheek. "Have fun," she said to Olivia before heading away, mobile phone in hand.

"You'll be okay," Abby said to her. "I'll look after you."

"I just… I don't—"

"It's okay."

The woman nodded and then turned to see someone being strapped onto the St Andrew's Cross. She let out an audible gulp.

Abby laughed. "It's not compulsory. See that woman over there?" Abby discreetly pointed to an older woman who had her back to them. "That's Jenny. She'd chew you up and spit you out." Abby laughed. "So we'll make sure you don't go anywhere near her." Abby felt the woman squeeze her hand tighter.

"Victoria said you're a journalist. Who do you write for?" Abby asked.

The woman looked at her and said nothing.

"Am I not supposed to know?" Abby asked. "I won't tell anyone."

"No, no, I'm not a journalist, I'm…"

Olivia stopped talking, her attention suddenly drawn to the other side of the room. She gasped. Abby followed her gaze, which seemed to have landed on Alison.

"That's Alison. That's who Victoria wants you to meet," Abby said, but she wasn't sure if Olivia had heard because she didn't acknowledge her. *I might as well be invisible,* Abby thought, then after a moment, Olivia nodded.

"Let me introduce you."

The woman again didn't say anything, but Abby took her silence as affirmation, and dragged her by the hand over to where Alison was chatting to someone with a large flogger.

"Victoria must think the two of you will get on," she said with a chuckle. "Alison."

Alison looked up, still running her hands over the length of the flogger.

"I'd like to introduce you to Olivia. Olivia, this is Alison. Alison, this is Olivia."

"Who?" Alison seemed to lose her grip on the leather, and

both Abby and the older chap Alison had been talking to bent forward to grab it, knocking their heads together.

"Olivia?" Alison peered intently at Olivia to a point where Abby wondered if she should point out that it's really rude to stare, even if she had been guilty of it herself when she first caught sight of Alison in her new domme attire.

Olivia nodded and raised her hand as though to lift her mask. Abby grabbed her hand.

"Masks must be kept on. It's a masquerade ball! You can take everything else off," Abby chuckled, "but masks must be kept on."

"Abby." Victoria approached them, clutching her phone, but she wasn't wearing the relaxed expression Abby had expected. Gareth was supposed to deliver good news, but her mistress didn't look at all happy. The graveness that etched over her features made Abby immediately drop her role as a sub.

"Victoria, is everything okay?" Abby knew that if all was well, then Victoria would immediately reprimand her for not calling her Mistress, but that didn't happen.

"I need you to come with me." Victoria grabbed her hand and pulled her away. "Alison, stay here."

Abby looked over her shoulder at the confused trio left behind, unsure of what was happening.

"Victoria. Stop. Talk to me." Abby stopped dead, halting Victoria's progress. It was only then did she register the look in her eyes. Panic.

"What did you and Alison do with the boxes?" Victoria's question came out in a high-pitched rush as Abby tried to understand the question.

"What boxes?"

"The boxes that came from UPS. The ones we thought Bryce had sent." Victoria stared directly into her eyes. "Abby, where are they?"

"In the viewing room. Alison thought the backroom was too crowded to hold more than the vacuum, so we moved them." Then she replayed exactly what Victoria had said. "What do you mean, the ones we *thought* Bryce had sent?" But Victoria was already tearing down the steps, heading for the large doors that led into the room which had been created for the viewing of live sex performances. Abby took off after her.

Victoria threw open the door with such force it clattered against the inner wall.

"Where is it?" she shouted.

"Over here." Abby flew by her shoulder, unsure of why the package was suddenly of such importance, unless... *Shit, no.*

The box lay open and empty apart from a she-wee, several small, empty plastic water bottles, and a few more filled with a dark yellow liquid. The box hadn't contained a toy; it had harboured a small, dehydrated woman.

"Fuck." Victoria glanced around the room. "The bitch is somewhere in here, and she's been here since yesterday."

Chapter 28
ALISON

Alison stared open-jawed at Victoria, who was leading Abby away by the hand. It was unlike Victoria to be so rude, so edgy, and a niggle of discomfort lodged in the pit of her stomach. But the command of *'Alison, stay here'* had rankled. Changing people's perception wasn't easy, especially when they'd already ensconced you in a nice, neat pigeon hole.

Tonight was her night to allow her internal changes to manifest themselves outwardly, hence the chaps and corset, but she knew all too well it wasn't clothes that made the domme. That came from within, an inner core of measured strength and a willingness to take a compassionate lead. Despite that, it was bloody hard to project that image when your ex-mistress was so blatantly giving you an order, right there in front of everyone.

Turning back to the half-naked woman in front of her, Alison tried desperately to assemble herself into the domme which matched her new attire, standing taller. The person she'd been so deeply in conversation with earlier, that had let her play with their flogger, had obviously sensed the vibe had changed and left. Alison was thankful it was now just the two of them.

"I like your daisies," she said. Even with the mask in place, Alison could feel her cheeks now redden. *I like your daisies. How lame was that for an opening line?* The cringe monster inside awakened, and she knew if she didn't do something fast, it would drain her of all the confidence she'd mustered. But it was Olivia who came to her rescue.

An inch shorter than Alison, Olivia moved closer, tilting her head up so she could whisper in her ear. "Can I tell you a secret?"

Olivia's breath tickled Alison's ear, and she half closed her eyes, revelling in the sensation.

"Victoria chose it for me. I think she wanted me gift wrapped so you couldn't say no."

"Victoria?" Alison turned to look at Olivia. "How do you know Victoria?"

Perhaps she shouldn't be surprised, after all Victoria seemed to know everyone, but Victoria had never mentioned Olivia.

"I'm ashamed to admit it, but I approached her."

Alison's brow creased in confusion. There were so many questions racing through her mind. *Why had Olivia contacted Victoria? Had they been discussing her without her knowing? What had been said?* She caught herself, forcing that line of thought from her head, refusing to allow the gremlins of paranoia space to grow. Not tonight. *But how had Olivia even found Victoria?*

Alison thought back to their therapeutic conversations. The rising chuckle came from the realisation that Alison had led Olivia right to Victoria. She'd told the woman everything. When they moved into the new house, the businesses they ran together, christ, she'd even told her about their daily habits. With that amount of information, even Clouseau could have found her. Alison started to speak, but before the first word was out, Olivia stopped her.

"Please don't say anything. I need to get this out. Lord knows, I've practised enough." Olivia's hand remained outstretched, halting Alison's questions. "I followed Victoria. I'm not proud of it, but I can't take it back now. Then I lied to her. I told her I was a journalist writing a story about dominatrixes. I used Jenny, too, to make the introduction. I wanted Victoria to teach me how to be a domme, and she had me do all this stuff and—"

Alison's confusion tinged with the red flare of anger. "Do what stuff? What did she make you do?"

That Olivia, *her Olivia*, had been made to do anything was intolerable to Alison.

"No. No, she didn't make me do anything. I used the wrong words. She suggested things to help me, and I chose to do them." Olivia's hands jittered in front of her. Alison's intervention obviously hadn't been part of whatever Olivia had practised, and the diversion from her plan was causing her to fluster. "She said to be a good domme, I had to be a good sub."

Alison's jaw dropped. What she was hearing was beyond awful. All she had wanted was someone of her own, to share that unique connection so many others took for granted, and now with the only person she'd ever thought there might be a sliver of a chance of realising that hope, she found Victoria had already claimed her. Her night couldn't get any worse.

"You and Victoria? You—" Alison couldn't, wouldn't, let the scenes which were playing in her head out into the bustle of the party. To say it out loud would make it real, and she wasn't ready to deal with the emotional discharge that would follow. Olivia's confession had the gravitas to alter her world. Tectonic plates shifting with such force that they'd change her emotional landscape beyond recognition…and this was happening in the frivolity of another bloody party? Fuck, she hated parties.

"No. Shit, I'm making such a fucking mess of this." Olivia grabbed her forehead with both hands, yanking her mask off. Alison barely registered the removal of the mask, too shocked by her words. She'd never heard Olivia swear before. "Victoria has never touched me, she's far too devoted to you to do that, but she helped me realise I don't have what it takes to be dominant in the bedroom, or anywhere, but if you're ever in the market for a sub that'll hang on your every command then…" Olivia gave a tight smile, her eyes full of hope, "I'd be up for the challenge."

Alison stood completely still. Over the course of the many, many hours she and Olivia had spent together, she had teased, coaxed, and flat out provoked the woman to get her to say these very words. Alison had imagined pulling her into a passionate kiss, allowing their bodies to meld together. But now, as fantasy and reality ploughed together, she was stunned.

"But if you don't want me, if I've got this wrong, again, then I can leave. I won't cause you any trouble." Olivia glanced over her shoulder as though she were desperate to locate the nearest exit. It was only as she made to turn away that Alison reached out. Taking hold of her arm, she spun Olivia round, then sliding one arm around her waist, she brought their bodies together.

"I want you." The corners of Alison's mouth twitched as she fought back a smile. Her lips had far better things to be doing right now.

From the moment their mouths met, the confusion of change evaporated, and for the first time, the cogs and gears seemed to work in harmony, creating balanced movement: this was her sub.

Chapter 29
VICTORIA

Victoria scanned the room, her eyes moving quickly, darting from one person to the next. There were so many people and, damn it, far too many tall people. She suppressed an urge to shout, *can everyone over 5' (in height) please lie down?* Seeing Abby standing on the spanking bench, Victoria asked, "Can you see her?"

"No, but I can see Bryce. He's—that's not important just now—but if you want to talk to him, he's behind the huge chap with the bald head on a stool."

"A bald man on a stool?" Victoria stood on her tiptoes looking for a fat, hairless man standing on a stool, but came up short.

"No, Bryce is on the stool." Abby jumped down. "Follow me."

Several seconds later, Victoria was face to side with Bryce, in full flow, completing a pelvic thrust that Tim Curry would have been proud of. She could only hope he remembered he was on a stool before he did a jump to the left.

"Bryce, how many parcels did you send?" Victoria wasn't

going to wait for Bryce to finish his routine. She needed answers, and she needed them now.

For a small man he was remarkably well endowed and Victoria couldn't help but wonder how he defied the laws of physics in remaining upright when excited. He turned to her, sweat beading his forehead.

"Fuck sake, Vicks. Slow down and inhale."

Clenching and unclenching her fist, she wondered how forceful a punch would be required to break the suction between Bryce and the big, bald bear, but Bryce seemed unaware of the danger he was in.

"Just answer my fucking question, Bryce." Whether it was her tone or the very fact that she was losing her cool, something that she never did, Bryce's rhythm seemed to falter, but he didn't stop.

It was only when Abby placed her hand on his forearm and said, "Bryce, have you been helping Mhairi? Was it you that organised Mhairi's box?" that he stopped dead.

A look of horror spread over his face, and Victoria thought he seemed to physically shrivel. She glanced down. He had.

"What the fuck?" Baldy shouted, craning behind from his bent position to see what was happening.

"Christ almighty, nothing can kill the moment like a fucking lesbian drama." Disengaging, he jumped off his stool and stared up at the two women. "Do I look like someone who would ever have anything to do with Mhairi's box?" With open palms he gestured to his small, half-naked body, half-covered in an outfit straight from *Elf*.

With arms crossed over their chests, both Victoria and Abby stared at him.

"You put Mhairi in a box and had her sent here by UPS. What the fuck were you thinking, Bryce? Where is she now?" Victoria's last ounce of patience evaporated. All she wanted was answers and to deal with Mhairi so that Alison could rebuild her life.

"I don't have a fucking clue where Mhairi is. I mailed Stefan." Bryce looked down, removing the loose latex from his earlier encounter.

"Stefan?" asked Victoria, screwing up her face. "Who's Stefan?"

Bryce rolled his eyes. "The sommelier with claustrophilia who had his way with the weightlifting—"

"Russian in the boot of that Fiat 500?" Victoria finished his sentence.

"See. You do know who Stefan is!" Bryce smiled as if everything in the world had gone back to normal...until he saw the big, bald bear blow a kiss to a leather clad chap with a set of steps. He was not a happy elf, Victoria mused, and then realised how grateful she was that she hadn't asked everyone over 5' to lie down.

"You gave him a she-wee to urinate in?" Victoria asked in confusion.

"Victoria." Abby took Victoria's hand. "Who cares? Mhairi isn't here."

Victoria shook her head. Letting out a long slow breath, relief flooded her system and emotions threatened to overwhelm as she was suddenly aware of the sting of tears. Until now, she hadn't acknowledged the silent stress of having Mhairi loose in the UK. Alison had made so much progress in the months that her ex had been gone, that to see it all destroyed now would be unthinkable. Victoria loved Alison to the very marrow of her bones. It differed from the feelings she had for Abby, just as deep, but less vehemently.

"Darling, are you okay?" Abby threw her arms around Victoria, pulling her head down onto her shoulder. Calling her *darling* had been a recent thing for Abby, but it gave Victoria a warm fuzzy feeling whenever she said it. Then, remembering where she was, and who she was, she straightened up again, quickly wiping away a stray tear before anyone could see.

"Bryce, I'm sorry we—interrupted you. It would appear we went off half-cocked." Victoria laid a hand on his shoulder and offered an apologetic smile.

"You and me both," he said in a forlorn tone as the big, bald bear secured the set of steps in place.

Chapter 30
ABBY

Victoria took Abby's hand and squeezed it tight. "You've done such an amazing job of organising tonight, you and Alison. I'm going to hire the pair of you for our corporate parties as well."

From the security of Victoria's lap, Abby glanced around the room. Callie, who seemed to be having a great deal of fun, was secured in the stocks, her wrists and neck resting on the padding, but locked into place with her arse in the air. A spreader attached to her ankles ensured everyone could see how much she was enjoying herself.

An older chap, whose name Abby didn't know, was secured to the St Andrew's Cross in the centre of the room. A slim woman wearing bright red PVC from head to toe was working at pace with a flogger. Abby watched as she inspected her handiwork, running fingertips over the red weals. As though sighing in disgust, the dominatrix flung the flogger down, disregarding it and replacing it with a much larger leather-handled bullwhip. The crack of the thick leather tail against flesh vibrated through Abby's body, and she squirmed.

"You like that?" Victoria asked, sliding her hand between Abby's legs. "I've not been giving you enough attention tonight," she murmured, allowing her fingertips to slide up the side of damp satin. "One day we might get you in the stocks," Victoria teased, but Abby knew exactly what she wanted.

"I want you to strap me to the cross. Tonight."

Victoria's eyes narrowed as though she was trying to work out if Abby was teasing her in return. But she dispelled that notion as she took Victoria's fingers, guiding them to her centre and popping open studs to give her mistress unfettered access. Having spent most of the evening ensuring everyone else was being looked after, there had been little time for the two of them to enjoy any of the entertainment. But finally, with refreshments flowing and the party in full swing, Victoria had secured the best viewing position on Alison's newest tantra chair. Having rested her back against the fuller of the two undulating curves, Victoria had kicked off her heels and pulled Abby down astride her lap.

Now, with fingers exploring her need, it was a position Abby was enjoying. She moaned, sliding against her mistress's fingers, bracing her hands against the smooth plum fabric. In the window's reflection, projected against the darkness of a rural Scottish night, she watched herself surrender to her lover's wishes. Victoria made her come alive; an instrument in a maestro's hands. Closing her eyes allowed the room to slide away so there was only one mistress remaining, that of desire.

"OMG! It's Santa."

Abby's eyes flew open, and sure enough, there was Santa on a quad bike approaching up the field, pulling a trailer holding Rudolph and two vertically challenged elves. The excited scream had come from a lanky, ginger man who, if Abby wasn't mistaken, was part of a Village People Tribute band that Matt had dragged her along to see; no two people could have pubes that violently ginger.

"I think we might have to pick this up later," Victoria whispered with an amused smile. Abby was never good at hiding her frustration.

Joining the others who were gathering around the open door to meet the man in red, they saw the motley crew make their way in. "Ho ho ho!" Santa bellowed.

"Did you arrange this?" Abby watched Victoria nod. "And you didn't tell me?"

Victoria shrugged, offering Abby a wicked grin. "You don't need to know everything. Plus, I like to surprise you."

Surprise was definitely the word Abby would have used when she saw what Santa was wearing under his big red suit. The red velvet mankini with strategically placed bubbles of white fluff raised a few whistles from the room. Thankfully, the rest of his squad remained in full costume.

Taking centre stage on the tantra chair where Abby had just been sitting with Victoria, Santa made himself comfortable as his elves dragged around the giant sacks.

"They have given me a nice list," he boomed, holding up a list of names, then placed a pair of black spectacles on his nose, "and a naughty list." The room erupted into laughter, with a few men and women claiming they had been very naughty indeed. "Only those on the naughty list get to sit on my knee."

While Abby cringed a little at his rhetoric, Santa was going down well with the rest of the room, and even better once the presents started flowing. Either Santa was reading the room well or Victoria had only handed over the names of those who she knew would respond well to a very non-PC Kris Kringle.

Jenny was one of those on the naughty list and she played along, revelling in the attention and securing herself a present of a tailoring session with Callie. As the two women made eye contact across the room, Abby realised there had only been one Secret Santa pulling the strings and that was Victoria.

Bryce followed, again on the naughty list, and Abby nearly wet herself when he unwrapped his gift to reveal a clear perspex chastity cage. It brought great hilarity but not as much raucous laughter as when one of the furry fetish guests started getting frisky with Rudolph, mounting the deer from behind. The back end of the outfit kicked furiously, but that made the entire spectacle more surreal. Victoria had to intervene to remind the chap this was a workplace for Rudolph and his very ample rump.

They gave several more gifts before it was Olivia's turn, and she looked delighted at being given a consultation for a new piece of furniture from Alison. From Alison's shocked expression, this was news to her, although, given the way they were looking at each other, Abby considered Victoria's penchant for present-giving to be en pointe.

Alison was on the nice list, being awarded with her own monogrammed set of crops, and Santa's sack was almost empty when Abby had her turn. She'd never enjoyed visiting the department store Christmas grottos as a kid, and going by how much her palms were sweating now, some things never changed. Her loud gasp of relief at being on the nice list brought laughter from the room, and when she opened her present, there were more than a few envious looks.

Neatly wrapped in tissue was a box containing a leather collar, cuffs (ankle and wrist), all of which bore Victoria's initials, and a silk blindfold. Made from Italian leather and backed with a soft velvet padding, Abby had never seen anything so beautiful.

"Thank you, Mistress," Abby said demurely, waiting for Victoria's nod so she could give her a hug. When she did,

Abby threw her arms around her neck and whispered in Victoria's ear, "Can we use them on the cross?"

"You want me to take you in front of everyone here, my Pet?"

Abby gave a slow nod. "I want you to show everyone you own me. That I'm yours and yours alone."

Abby had a thrill of excitement when Victoria grasped her chin, looked into her eyes and simply said, "Your cunt is mine."

That one line left her wide-eyed and panting. Victoria had never talked to her like that before and, *hell, that was hot.*

"I've one more gift left, and you are a lucky girl, Alison, because this one's for you as well. What did you do that was so good I have rewarded you with two presents this year?" Santa raised his eyebrows, holding out a beautifully wrapped gift in a matte gold paper with a black bow.

Victoria's head snapped around to stare at the muscled man in the mankini holding the gift. Her perplexed expression immediately told Abby what was happening now wasn't by Victoria's construct.

Alison, though, didn't seem to share any of Victoria's concern, happily striding towards Santa with her hand out.

"Ooh, your fur's so soft…" Mr Fur-Fetish was rubbing his hands over Rudolph's rump again, grabbing everyone's attention, so not everyone saw the colour drain from Alison's face after she ripped off the paper and saw the *gift.*

Abby's jaw dropped. A leather collar bearing the monogram MD rested in Alison's hand. MD for Mhairi Dunlop. Victoria's eyes darted around the room and Abby stepped towards Alison. As more people turned their focus back to Alison, a hush fell over the room. Only Mr Fur-Fetish seemed oblivious to the distress, unable to hold back his incessant stroking. Eventually Rudolph's arse, pushed beyond its limits, let rip.

"Will you fuck off?" The aggressive low pitch of the voice was unmistakable, and before Victoria could react, Rudolph's arse detached itself from the rest of the body and stood up... Standing at her full 4' 10", was a ruddy-faced Mhairi with brown furry legs and braces holding them in place. Abby had a strange combination of fear and an irrational need to giggle when she saw the resemblance to her favourite character from *The Lion, The Witch and The Wardrobe.* Mhairi was an overweight embodiment of Mr Tumnus. Even her ears stuck out in the right places thanks to her head being placed next to someone's bottom for an hour.

"Well, hello, Alison." Mhairi's voice dripped with contempt.

Chapter 31
ALISON

Instinctively, Alison stepped in front of Olivia, who had run to her side when she had seen the collar.

"What do you want?" Alison's eyes darted around the room, looking for Victoria, her protector.

"I thought I'd drop by and say hello, see how you were getting on. I mean, I would be a terrible mistress if I didn't check in on my sub, wouldn't I? And who's this we have here?" Mhairi stepped forward, approaching Olivia. "Have you got me a new recruit? How thoughtful." Mhairi reached out, allowing one finger to stroke Olivia's pale skin.

Alison froze, unable to comprehend what was happening. *No, she couldn't have Olivia. There's no way she would let her get near Olivia.*

"Take your hands off her," Alison said, trying to reassert herself between the two women.

"Down, slut. I can see you need to learn your place. Do you think you put on some black leather and become me? I don't think so."

"I never want to be you," Alison said vehemently, suddenly aware that everyone had their eyes on her, waiting for her next move. Again she looked to Victoria, but this time it wasn't with a plea for help. It was an assertive nod to let her know she had this. "What do you want, Mhairi?" Alison's tone was steady, dispassionate.

"I'm here for what is rightfully mine, and that includes you, this delightful new woman, and the contents of your bank account. We're leaving tonight and you're coming with me," Mhairi sneered, causing Alison's stomach to retch. How had she ever allowed this woman to touch, let alone…

Mhairi grabbed the unlit cigarette that Mr Fur-Fetish was holding.

"I wouldn't do that if I were you," he said, reaching to claw it back, but Mhairi was too quick. In one swift movement, she placed the cigarette in her lips and leant, lifting a candle to the end and inhaling. A huge flame sparked in front of her face, and with eyes as wide as saucers, she blew it out, stumbling slightly. Alison watched as Mr Fur-Fetish dropped his head into his hands, laughing, not understanding what had just happened, but she didn't have time to dwell on it because from that moment someone pressed fast-forward and everything in her life became fluid.

It started with Abby saying, "I think you'll find that you can't smoke in this house," and was rapidly followed by Mhairi lurching forward, reaching out as though she were trying to put her hand under Olivia's chin.

"You're nothing but a slut. You were a poor excuse for a sub and you don't exist without me. I know because I broke you, just like I'll break this pretty little Daisy, too." Mhairi's words were slurred, but every insult cut into Alison like the knife wounds they were. She felt panic rise through her body, the conflict between the hate-filled diatribe from the woman she'd obeyed for the last ten years, and saving Olivia was all-consuming.

Out of the corner of her eye, Alison saw Victoria's

flaming red hair fly across the room and she knew what she had to do. This was her fight, and this was where she had to make her stand, not just to save Olivia, but to save herself, too.

The reel swapped from fast-forward to slo-mo. Pulling back her right arm, twisting her body, and throwing her weight from back foot to front, Alison landed a single powerful hook that sent Mhairi's head flying both up and back. The furry brown legs elevated above the flagstone floor as Mhairi's back arched as though she were in an Olympic high jump event, and then, as time squirrelled forward, she went straight down with an almighty *thump*.

Nobody moved.

"Has Rudolph's butt just died?" Mr Fur-Fetish gave a giddy scream.

It was Victoria who dropped beside Mhairi's apparently lifeless body, carefully placing two fingers to the side of her neck. Alison watched, horrified, when Victoria adjusted the position of her fingers. She hadn't meant to…

A gush of vomit spewing over Victoria's black patent heels followed the initial cough.

"Fucking really?" Victoria stood, kicking off orange lumps of sickness from her feet. "Somebody help me put her in the recovery position before she chokes to death on her own vomit. Why the fuck is there always carrots?"

"We are talking about Rudolph," Bryce said, coming to her help, and they rolled her onto her side, bending one knee to keep her in position.

"What the fuck was in that cigarette?" Victoria glared at Mr Fur-Fetish, who brought out a little brown bottle from his pocket, waving it in glee. The label said, *Leather Polish.*

"Butyl Nitrate. Poppers," Bryce explained. "They soak a cigarette in it and then they can sniff or smoke. You've got a zero tolerance on drugs, so this way they can have their fun and you're none the wiser." Bryce shrugged, as though what he was saying was common knowledge. "She's passed out. Give her a few minutes and she'll be right as rain again, but probably more feisty than before. I hope you're ready for it."

Alison scanned the room, looking for something to tie Mhairi's hands and feet. There was no way she was letting this woman near Olivia. There were ropes, handcuffs, zip ties. Every sort of restraint you could imagine was in this room. But then she had a thought.

"Don't let her get up." Alison ran from the room, returning a minute later with Bryce's latex vacuum frame. "We can use this."

Victoria shot her a look of alarm, but Bryce just shrugged. "It'd do the trick," he said.

A few snickers of laughter tickled the room as Mhairi moaned and flailed her arms.

"We need to get her in it now if we're going to do this or we'll end up sitting on her until the police arrive." Alison held open the side, ready to receive Mhairi's body.

Bryce grabbed Mhairi's legs, sliding them into the large latex envelope, but Victoria didn't follow suit.

"C'mon, Victoria," Alison hissed, watching Victoria's eyes dart between the two of them.

"You're absolutely sure she won't suffocate? I don't want her to die by our hands."

Bryce rolled his eyes. "We'll make sure she can breathe. I can make the breathing hole bigger so her entire face is uncovered and we'll only vacuum it enough to restrict her movement. Trust me, I've been doing this for years and I've never lost anyone yet."

Alison was relieved to see Victoria nod, and then with a rough shove, guided Mhairi's full body under the latex. The vacuum was pumping out the last of the air when Mhairi became fully roused and she writhed against the latex in the tiniest bit of wiggle room they had left her. Her 4'10" frame suctioned into place by the black latex made Mhairi's body appear like a 3D model of the Lake District.

"Get me out of this. Fucking get me out of this or I'll kill you all," Mhairi screamed, her face turning puce, entirely from rage. "Oh—oh—fuck! What the fuck have you done to me?"

Victoria held the back of her hand up to her nose, wincing from the rising stench.

"Yeah," Bryce grimaced, "apart from fainting, loss of bowel control is a bit of a kicker, too."

The entire room all backed away in unison, groaning as their faces took on varying degrees of contortion. All except Alison, who laughed, and continued to laugh as Victoria glared at her.

"What? Oh, come on. You're not going to tell me this isn't karma?" Alison said with a grin.

"This is a natural stone floor with a heated underlay. If any of her—fluids—leak, it'll cost a fortune to have it cleaned. We'll need one of those crime scene cleaners you see on TV."

Ten minutes later, two chaps from the security firm Victoria had hired closed the back of the van doors. Mhairi, her fluids, and the latex frame had all been secured in place, and were now en route to Gayfield Police Station in Edinburgh, and as luck would have it, not one inch of stone floor was damaged.

Chapter 32
VICTORIA

Victoria had just finished quizzing Santa about his hiring policy when Bryce appeared, dousing himself in sanitiser.

"What did Santa have to say for himself?" Pulling out the waistband of his tight red leather shorts, he scooshed the sanitiser down the gap, wincing as it hit the spot. "What?" he asked, catching Victoria's look of despair. "I've got to keep it fresh."

Victoria rolled her eyes, not for the first time that night. "Mhairi was a last-minute replacement when his other rump, a girl called Darian, phoned in sick." They exchanged knowing glances. "Jenny's mortified to have been harbouring a traitor all this time. It seems for Darian, it's a case of once Mhairi's sub, always Mhairi's sub. She gave Mhairi every bit of information she needed to gain access. I doubt anyone will touch her with a barge pole now, though."

"Little bitch," Bryce muttered, allowing his gaze to follow Santa.

Victoria knew she'd lost him to the big guy. He had no attention span if there was a six-pack floating about. The evening's impromptu entertainment hadn't seemed to dampen spirits, much to her relief. If it had ended like the last one, she, Abby, and Alison would be social pariahs on the kink circuit. But as luck would have it, Alison and her single deftly delivered blow had secured their position, and raised Alison's standing to become the hottest new domme on the scene. The journey she'd taken had been brutal, but often the longest, hardest routes develop the most compassionate travellers, and Victoria knew Alison would be a remarkable domme.

The vibrations emanating from the phone she gripped tightly in her hand stopped Victoria's reflections dead. This was the call she'd been waiting for.

"Gareth, did you get the package?"

That the girl Victoria had saved from Mhairi's clutches was the one who had betrayed them had left her a little unsettled, she knew the security firm whose operatives had left with Mhairi were solid. She'd vetted them herself, but she'd thought the same thing when she'd hired Santa and his crew. In short, she wouldn't rest until she heard Gareth's answer.

"We've spent the last ten minutes out in the yard hosing her down. She was making one hell of a dirty protest. I'll be lucky if I can get the smell of shit out of my nose before Christmas dinner."

Victoria laughed. "Any excuse to avoid the brussel sprouts."

Gareth gave a grunt that suggested he'd run with that idea and asked Victoria if she wanted to come in to make a statement. She declined the offer. There were more than enough charges piling up against the woman without them having to be involved. They had both businesses and reputations to protect. Mhairi was going down; there was no reason for them to be associated with the unsavoury publicity the woman created.

Gareth would get a feather in his cap for picking up Mhairi. Victoria had arranged for the vacuum-packed domme to be delivered to the edge of the square opposite the police station. Once in position, the boys were to wait until they were sure that Gareth had her under arrest. Nobody needed to know how it had happened. Victoria wished him a happy Christmas for when the time came, and turned her attention back to the party. There was one promise she was yet to keep.

Chapter 33
VICTORIA

Heading back into the house, the party seemed to be a little subdued. "Come on, everybody. This is a party and I apologise for the inconvenience and interruption we had earlier, but it's Christmas. Come on."

Somebody turned up the music and the sound of crops hitting warm flesh filled the room again.

"Are you okay?" Victoria said to Alison.

"I'm so very okay." Alison nodded, sliding her arm over Olivia's shoulders. "And I don't know how this happened, not properly." Alison passed a glance between Victoria and Olivia. "And I'm sure I'll find out, but thank you."

"Sometimes things just need a gentle push." Victoria smiled and shrugged, grateful that they had finally got together.

"If you don't mind, we'll stay for another couple of drinks and then head back to the main house." Alison nodded towards the larger house next door, which held all the sleeping and living accommodation.

"Absolutely." Turning her attention to Olivia, Victoria asked, "Have you enjoyed yourself? It hasn't been too overwhelming, I hope?" Victoria watched as Olivia slipped her hand into Alison's so she was practically hugging Alison's side.

"It's been interesting,"—she chuckled—"but Alison has kept me safe."

The squeeze of the fingers was almost imperceptible, but Alison's chest swelling with pride gave the game away, and Victoria couldn't be happier for them. But she had someone of her own she should look out for.

"Have you seen Abby?" Victoria's eyes scoured the room.

"Over there." Alison pointed towards the Christmas tree, and sure enough, there she was, deep in conversation with Matt. She grabbed herself a drink from the tray of champagne flutes the waiter was carrying and made her way across.

"And what are you two plotting?"

They both looked up with very guilty expressions, but Victoria chose not to probe. Tonight had already had too much drama, but whatever covert operations they were putting in place, Matt didn't seem to want to discuss them in front of Victoria and made a polite exit. Victoria didn't complain.

"Have you got your present from Santa handy, my Pet?" Victoria watched Abby glance over to the St Andrew's Cross which dominated the room, her eyes sparkling in anticipation.

"I have them right here, Mistress." Abby held them up, and Victoria took them from her grasp. Their fingers grazed, and she saw her own jolt of desire reflected in the darkened eyes of her sub.

"With me, now."

Victoria picked up the Coco de Mer black, braided leather crop—her favourite. But it appeared that she wasn't the only one intent on pleasuring their sub, as Nylon Norman was also heading for the cross with Matt in tow.

"I think not, Norman." Victoria blocked him. Then using the flattened end of the crop, she pushed Abby against the cross. "I want you facing me."

Victoria's breathing grew shallower as she watched her younger sub stretch her limbs out, ready to be restrained. The collar looked exquisite around her neck, as though it had always belonged there. Taking her time, Victoria secured one wrist and then the next, sliding her body against the hot flesh she was about to devour.

Allowing her tongue to trail down Abby's cleavage, she squeezed her breasts, revelling in the soft moan her actions elicited. With her goal in mind, she continued on languidly, making her way down to secure her ankles, pausing only briefly to inhale her pet's excitement. This was what she had been waiting for, not just tonight but since she had taken Abby for that very first time. Patience and nurturing had brought them to this point, and while this had always been *her* chosen destination, she'd waited for Abby to be ready to make that choice…and tonight, she had chosen.

With the last click of metal, her beautiful sub was ready. Victoria pressed herself against Abby, allowing her hands to run over her thighs, warming the pale flesh that was about to quiver by her command.

"Safe word," Victoria demanded, allowing her fingertips to slide over the damp satin between Abby's legs.

"Fray Bentos." The quiver in her pet's voice brought a slow smile to her face. Tonight, she would claim Abby, as her own, in front of everyone.

"If I go too fast—Amber. Okay?" Victoria stared deep into Abby's blue eyes, which were darkening by the moment. Satisfied that her young lover's skin was warm enough, she stepped back, allowing the flat tip of the crop to trace small circles over her thighs. Abby would see every rise and fall of the leather, hear every swish of the crop before the crack as it made contact with her thigh.

"I want you to look straight at me." Victoria settled her gaze on Abby's face. "Don't close your eyes, don't look away, don't look at the crop."

"Yes, Mistress."

Victoria, unblinking, stepped back. The only sound in the room was her own slow, measured breathing, now heavy with desire. Lifting her arm, she readied herself and then, with one quick flick of her wrist, she brought leather and flesh together. Abby winced, but didn't break eye contact. "Again?" Victoria asked.

The slow nod and smile granted her permission, and she brought the crop down again, and again, in quick succession. The skin around Abby's jaw tightened, but still she stared straight at her mistress. With an almost imperceptible nod, she asked for more, and Victoria didn't hold back. Changing her stance, the leather found virgin skin. She'd done this exact same thing with many other subs, but never with Abby. The rush of her pulse filled her ears, and her heart thundered with arousal. God, how long had she wanted Abby like this? Power versus surrender. Dominatrix and devoted pet.

Several evenly dispersed cracks later and her pet was fighting pleasure so strong her lids had become heavy. Victoria knew she wanted nothing more than to surrender, the buzz of arousal filling her body. They were so close.

"Look at me."

Abby forced her eyes open. Victoria moved forward, allowing her crop to fall to the floor and ran her palms, now warm with exertion, over the red stripes on Abby's thighs. Never had she wanted anyone to surrender to her so completely.

"I'm going to take you. Claim you, as mine, with everyone

watching." Victoria moved her head, indicating the small circle of people that gathered around them. "Every one of them will watch you surrender to me, and only me."

For the first time, Abby's gaze broke away, taking in their audience.

"Eyes on me." Victoria ran her fingers ever closer to Abby's centre, then without warning she pulled apart the studs which kept the underside of the briefs in place, exposing her completely. There were murmurs of appreciation, but Victoria had a rush of exhilaration knowing that she controlled Abby's pleasure.

A whimper broke from Abby's chest as Victoria slid her fingers down either side of her swollen clit.

"You can't come until I give you permission."

Abby groaned, pulling against the restraints, desperately trying to grind herself harder against her mistress's touch, but each time she moved, Victoria eased her fingers away. Since Abby's punishment session, Victoria had reset the rules as her mistress, taking firm control with her pet, but today she'd take her to the very edge, allowing her the choice of ultimate surrender.

Victoria reached into the top of her corset and pulled out a tiny finger vibrator. The very latest in stimulation from her supplier. Slipping it onto the tip of her thumb, she lowered her hand and ran the silicon through Abby's wetness, coating it in the young woman's juices. The way Abby squirmed under her touch drove her on, teasing the thousands of nerve endings in her clit, then around and in her velvety smooth entrance.

Her pet's body writhed between the cross and the weight of Victoria's body, wrists and ankles pulling against the tight constraints. The rush of power was intoxicating, and Victoria never wanted this euphoria to end.

"Please…" Abby's plea did nothing to hide her abject want.

"Not yet."

Abby's eyes widened, her mouth falling open. Victoria knew she was clinging on by her fingernails. Abby was so close to where she wanted her to be…just a little more. Sliding fingers deep inside, Victoria allowed the tiny vibrator attached to her thumb to roll over Abby's engorged clit.

"Please…" Abby whined, her breathing coming in gasps.

"If I allow you to come, what will you give me?" Victoria's gaze bore deep into Abby's soul, stripping away everything that had ever stood between them, until there was only the mistress and her pet. Dominant and submissive.

"E-everything." Abby's voice broke and her eyes were wet with tears. "Everything, Mistress."

Victoria inhaled deeply, savouring the moment. To the uninitiated, it might seem that she was controlling the woman she loved with simple tiny movements of her fingertips. But the complete surrender Abby was giving her, her mistress, was an accumulation of respect, honesty, choice and consent, and underpinning it all, love.

"Marry me." Victoria swallowed, a rush of emotion cascading through her body. "Please, marry me."

"Yes. God, yes!" Abby's eyes glinted with tears of happiness as she broke into a huge smile.

"You have no idea how much I love you," Victoria whispered in her ear, her voice breaking with emotion, as she clasped her lover, their bodies spasming into orgasm.

Chapter 34
ALISON

"So where's the wedding going to be?" Alison placed her drink on the acacia coffee table. The ice chinked against the glass and a tiny drop of Glayva splashed her hand. Instinctively, she lifted it to her lips, only to be stopped by Olivia.

"Let me get that for you." There was a seductive glint in Olivia's eyes as she popped Alison's finger into her mouth and sucked.

Alison let her eyes close slowly, relishing the wave of desire rising in her body. They had hardly kept their hands off each other since the night of the party, despite promises of taking it slow.

Lucas cleared his throat.

"Anyone for more wine?" Victoria brandished the bottle of Barolo, glancing around the room at everyone's glasses.

"Not for me." Lucas placed his hand over the glass, ensuring Victoria didn't have the option to top it up.

Olivia rolled her eyes, and Alison gave her a sly smile. Inviting Lucas had been at Victoria's insistence. Over the last week, Olivia had spent most evenings (and nights) with them at the farmhouse, and Alison made no secret of the fact she

186

wanted Olivia with them to share Christmas. The only crease in the plan was that Olivia usually spent the day with Lucas, given they were both on their own for the holidays. So Victoria decided the more the merrier, and they had extended the invite to Lucas. Alison was grateful for Victoria's generosity, as was Olivia, but Lucas wasn't a straightforward character to read.

Alison found him a little standoffish, verging on geeky, but Olivia assured her he just viewed the world a little different from most people, and because of that, the world viewed him a little differently, too. Alison didn't disagree.

"I wouldn't mind a top-up." Matt held his glass aloft, waving it precariously in the air.

The intercom buzzed, declaring they had a guest arriving, and Victoria glanced over her shoulder towards the kitchen which still housed security screens.

"Here, let me." Alison took the bottle from Victoria, who was standing on the opposite side of the table, and poured a generous glug into his glass. "Anyone else?"

"Jenny's here," Victoria announced, touching the release control for the gates.

With no takers, Alison sat down, placing a protective arm around Olivia's shoulders. The reassuring ping from the kitchen told her the electric gates had closed behind Jenny's vehicle and the perimeter had been secured. Alison almost chuckled, *the perimeter secured*. The thought deserved a place in an FBI thriller rather than a Christmas Day celebration with friends, but the security system itself was a stark reminder of Mhairi and the turmoil she'd brought to all their lives, but mostly to Alison herself.

With Mhairi now safely incarcerated in HMP Cornton Vale, awaiting her extradition hearings (which everyone knew to be a foregone conclusion), they could all breathe a little easier. It would be simple for Alison to brush that period of her life under the carpet, to wish she'd never clapped eyes on the woman, but her work with Olivia had made her realise that this was a journey she'd chosen to travel. Ownership for her part in what had transpired was allowing her to heal. Not that she was taking on account-ability for Mhairi's abuse, because that was her abuser's cross to bear. By understanding her own actions and motivations, it allowed her to make better choices for today. Besides, if she had never met Mhairi, then she'd never have met Olivia, and sitting with the warmth of her lover's body snuggled against her own, that was unthinkable.

There were fatalists who might argue that Olivia was always destined to be in her future regardless of the path she'd taken to reach that point, but Alison didn't share their view of the world. Life was all about choice.

The same way it had been Olivia's choice to report herself to her professional board. The Monday following the party, she had resigned her post within the practice, offered a full and frank disclosure of her actions, and recused herself from practising psychotherapy. Alison had tried to slow her down, fearing it was a knee-jerk reaction which she'd come to regret. After all, neither Alison nor Victoria were ever going to disclose the background to their relationship, but Olivia couldn't live with herself. She had made a mistake, a heinous error of judgement proving she was just as flawed as many of the people who she helped. She was human.

As Olivia explained, her decision was born out of respect for her other patients, as well as Alison. Her clients needed somebody who would always put their care first, above everything, and they needed to start their relationship without lies or secrets. It had to be based on respect, honesty, choice, and consent. The four pillars.

Dr Olivia Hopkins was now just Olivia, ready to start a new chapter in her life. They were still very much at the beginning of their journey, both charting unfamiliar territory, but together. Neither of them knew what lay ahead, but for Alison, there was a surety in her heart that she'd found her person.

It wasn't a feeling she could explain in words, because it wouldn't fit into anything as mundane or structured as a sentence. Not even a paragraph or a book would do it justice. What she had with Olivia differed from anything she'd experienced before. A living, breathing, dynamic connection that was both scary and exciting at the same time. She smiled to herself, turning and placing a small kiss on the side of Olivia's forehead. There was so much to be grateful for already, and even more adventures for them in the future, including Victoria and Abby's wedding. Now that was going to be quite an event.

"Christmas Charades!" Abby declared as she walked into the room.

Alison and everyone else seated around the room gave a collective groan, rubbing their full bellies as though all they wanted to do was sit quietly and contemplate as their food digested, all except Matt. The two of them had declared themselves the entertainment queens, with Matt even donning a bright red blazer to ensure he fully played his part.

"It's like charades but with a twerk." Matt winked at Lucas, who seemed to disappear farther into the sofa.

"Did somebody say charades?" Jenny appeared in a spangle of sequins, armed with a scotch over ice. After spending the day with her son, his wife, and her four grandchildren, she had the look of a woman ready to dive right into the festivities.

"There are two themes," said Abby, so excited she was almost jumping on the spot, "some are festive and some are fetish." A wicked grin tugged up the corners of her mouth. "And you don't get to choose before you ask."

Alison watched as Lucas closed his eyes. The poor man didn't know what he'd let himself in for, but she wasn't the only one who had seen his reaction.

"My dear fellow, you look as though you are ready to pass out." Jenny sidled between their feet and the coffee table, saying to Olivia and Lucas, "Room for a small one in the middle?"

The fact her question was rhetorical was obvious as she squeezed her ample behind between them on the sofa, making everyone laugh.

"I'm Jenny," she said to a startled looking Lucas, "but you can call me your guardian angel. I'm making it my personal mission to take care of you tonight." Squeezing his knee, she offered him a lascivious smile. His gulp was audible.

This is family, Alison thought, watching everyone laugh. They were just a normal family celebrating together—well, as long as you considered nipple clamps normal.

Oh wait, before you go!

I hope you enjoyed getting to know Kristi & Fenna.

The Healing Hearts series is just beginning, so if you would like to follow along,

please sign up to my newsletter

Your Words

are as important to an author

as an author's words

are to you.

CLICK HERE

Please leave me a review

Love Ruby x

Thank you to...

As an indie author readers often think the entire process is down to the author, but the success of a book is down to the team that surrounds them. In this respect I am lucky. I have an exceptional bunch of humans (and one wee furry girl) who help make every publication possible.

Thank you to; **Angie** (my wife and marketing manager), **Lisa, Jayne and Monna** (my Beta Readers), my **ARC Team**, you all know who you are, and **Bailey**, my furry inspiration who listens to me cuss in frustration and then gives me a cuddle.

And thank you to you, for taking the time and making the effort to find and read my books. I hope they make you smile.

About Ruby Scott

Ruby Scott lives in a quiet village nestled in the Scottish hills with her wife, Angie, and their furry little girl, Bailey. As an avid reader she got up one day, had an extra cup of coffee, and thought, I'm going to write a book.

It's amazing where an extra cup of coffee can take you. Endless curiosity combined with a love of traveling and books, Ruby is never without adventure.

It's an adventure everyone is welcome to join.

Also by Ruby Scott

Also by Ruby Scott

Stronger You Series

Inside Fighter

Seconds Out

On The Ropes

Evergreen Series

Evergreen

The Velvet Storm Series

The Stranger Within Me

Strangely Familiar

Ruby Scott

www.rubyscott.com

Printed in Great Britain
by Amazon